Advance Praise

"David Metz's compassionate vision shows us ordinary people trying to keep their resilience and their dignity as they roll with the punches of life. Without false sentiment, these stories affirm that we are mostly decent people trying to be better, and often succeeding, despite our foolishness and mistakes. It's a pleasure to read such finely tuned, insightful fiction."

> — J. Morris, author of *When I Snap My Fingers You Will Remember Everything*

"There are no gimmicks in this exceptional collection of stories written with a clear-eyed understanding of the way our own decisions, regrets, desires, and hopes, and those of the people we encounter along the way, loom over our lives for better and for worse. These characters feel like friends and relatives, past and present, a family or regional history of fully imagined, flesh and blood people pushing themselves toward and away from each other for good and bad reasons they mostly don't quite comprehend until damage is done and fates are sealed. Just like real life. A sparkling debut collection whose characters will stick with you long after you've put the book down."

> — Dave Housley, author of *The Other Ones, Looney, This Darkness Got to Give*, and others

"A collection of elegant and open-hearted stories."

— Kirkus Reviews

Nick and Lorraine
Were Lovers

Nick and Lorraine
Were Lovers

David C. Metz

Apprentice
House Press
Loyola University Maryland

First Edition

Library of Congress Control Number: 2025932560

Casebound ISBN: 978-1-62720-581-8
Paperback ISBN: 978-1-62720-582-5
Ebook ISBN: 978-1-62720-583-2

Cover & Internal Design by Molly Clement
Editorial Development by Matthew McCarney
Promotional Development by Olivia DiTroia

Published by Apprentice House Press

Apprentice
House Press
Loyola University Maryland

Loyola University Maryland
4501 N. Charles Street, Baltimore, MD 21210
410.617.5265
www.ApprenticeHouse.com
info@ApprenticeHouse.com

For Susan

Previous Publication Acknowledgements

Nick and Lorraine Were Lovers – The MacGuffin

Knowing – Valparaiso Fiction Review

A Place to Be – Adelaide Literary Magazine

Everything Will Be Fine – Bull

Objects in Motion – New Plains Review

Changing Colors – District Lit

Old Man Murphy's Boy – BoomerLitMag

Death by Ferris Wheel – The Oddville Press

Her Brother's Keeper -- Vita Poetica

No One Left Behind – Perceptions Magazine

The Hat – Blue Lake Review

Contents

Nick and Lorraine Were Lovers

Petrocelli's fist caught Nick square on the nose and nearly knocked him to the sidewalk. Blinking back tears as the initial sting gave way to a deep throb, he covered his nose with his right hand and held his left in the direction of Petrocelli, palm out, like a cop halting traffic. They were in front of a restaurant called Tully's on a Sunday morning in April. A couple on their way inside slowed their pace and turned their heads in Nick's direction, like drivers passing a car crash. Inside, a few people were staring out from under the capital "T" stenciled in green on the front window.

"Jesus, son," Petrocelli said. "Are you okay?" He was a little over six feet, the same height as Nick, but had the solid frame of a man who did physical labor and made Nick feel skinny, insubstantial. Petrocelli stared at him, looking surprised and a little stricken at the damage he had done.

"Of course he's not okay. He's bleeding. Did you have to hit him so hard?" Lorraine stepped towards Nick, who had turned sideways and bent slightly at the waist. "I think it will be better if you can stand straight and tilt your head back. Can you do that?"

Nick straightened as Lorraine stepped closer, her green eyes studying his nose. She put her hands on his shoulders.

"Let me see."

Nick moved his hand from his nose to see it was covered in blood that ran down to his wrist. "Shit."

1

"It's broken." Lorraine shot a quick glance at Petrocelli. "We need to take him to the hospital, babe. Can you get the car?"

Still staring at Nick, Petrocelli nodded, took one step backwards, then another, slowly unsticking himself from the scene.

"I'm fine," Nick said, wincing.

Lorraine shook her head. "No, you're not." She gripped his arms gently and looked at him. "Don't move, okay? Just stand right here." She hurried back inside.

Nick looked at the people staring out the window and nodded. They responded by moving away, as if suddenly realizing it was not a one-way window like on TV police procedurals.

When Lorraine reappeared, she held a wet white washcloth folded into a square. "Hold this against your nose and keep your head back." She looked at him, tilting her head to one side and then the other, trying to find the best angle of view. "Jesus, Nick," she finally said.

The cold cloth felt good but made his nose sting and eyes water when he pressed too hard. Head back, he stared at Lorraine through blurry eyes for the second time in 24 hours. He told her the same thing as before. "He doesn't love you." But his voice sounded nasally and thin and robbed the words of his intended effect. Lorraine was trying not to laugh.

"I'm sorry," she said. "I know it's not funny. But if you could see yourself."

He should have been upset, but there was something about Lorraine that kept him off balance, caused him to react in unexpected ways. He had known her for four months, yet it seemed longer, and she seemed older, even though at twenty-one, she was just two years older than him. They'd met in an Introduction to Philosophy class when she took the seat next to his. He noticed her small hands as she gripped her pen almost childlike, with her thumb pressed against the knuckle of her index finger. Periodically, she pushed a long strand of brown hair out of her face without shifting her focus from her notes or the professor. At the end of class, she turned to him.

"It's rude to stare."

He started to speak, stopped, shook his head. "Sorry." He smiled, hoping she wouldn't walk away before he could think of something to keep the conversation going. He watched her button her coat, put on a knit cap, and sling her back-pack over her shoulder before turning to him.

"Did you want to ask me for a cup of coffee or something?"

He noticed that her smile was lopsided, the right side of her mouth lifting slightly higher than the left, eyes crinkled, an expression that disarmed Nick as completely as the contours of her body beneath blue jeans and a cashmere sweater.

She was the first woman he had seen completely naked. His nighttime explorations in the backseat of his father's car had been more tactile than visual: clothing unbuttoned or unzipped, pushed up or tugged down to reveal partial views of breasts and thighs and the curve of hips. Nick was not a virgin the first time Lorraine took him to her small off-campus apartment, but he may as well have been. He had rehearsed the moment, wanting to be cool, but standing in the middle of the room with the light on and all that space as she nonchalantly undressed, left him dumbfounded.

They saw each other every day, and Nick spent most nights at her apartment. His roommate grinned and shook his head when Nick stopped by the residence hall to change clothes or pick up a text book. It was intended as a compliment, but made Nick feel defensive. He couldn't treat Lorraine like found money.

He told her he wanted to do something with his life, not just grind out a living. Maybe something to do with the environment, although he wasn't particularly good in science. But he could write and thought he could help raise awareness, be an activist or an investigative journalist. He told her about books and movies he liked, and places he wanted to see. She listened and smiled and revealed little about herself. He began to think she was protecting some secret, a vulnerability, and it aroused in him a desire to protect her. He wondered if she lacked confidence, even though in class she didn't hesitate to ask questions, while Nick hung back, thinking he should know the answers. But there were different kinds of confidence.

Once he asked her what she wanted, she laughed and said "you." They were sitting on the sofa in her apartment, late-afternoon light filtering through the half-opened venetian blinds.

"No, I mean in life. What do you want to do?"

She gave him a quizzical look. "I don't know. Get a good job."

"Is that all?"

She nudged him with her elbow. "We can't all save the world, Nick."

"I'm serious."

"I know. Sometimes you're too serious."

"Does it bother you?"

She shook her head, smiling. "No, I think it's sweet."

"Sweet?"

"Kind of."

"So, what do you want?"

She laughed again. "I don't know, Nick, what does anyone want? To be happy, right?"

He started to speak but she pressed a finger to his lips and stood, pulling him to his feet. As he followed her down the hall he thought, *maybe she is found money.*

• • •

Nick rode in the backseat on the way to the hospital. Lorraine sat in the front next to Petrocelli, half turned in her seat so she could look at Nick and give his knee a reassuring squeeze. Petrocelli glanced at Nick through the rearview mirror. His blue eyes, set deep in a round face, betrayed little, but his voice, gravelly and hoarse, as if his vocal chords had been permanently scratched, carried a note of concern. "Hang in there."

"We'll be there in five minutes," Lorraine said.

Nick nodded. When he was twelve, he broke his thumb playing Pop Warner football and rode from the game to the emergency room with an ice bag on his hand while his parents' solicitous comments only made him feel worse. The memory sent a needle of pain through his septum.

• • •

Lorraine waited until the end to tell him about Petrocelli. They were spooning, his head resting on her shoulder.

"I love you," he said.

"Hmmm," she murmured. "I know what you love, and it isn't me."

"I do love you, Lorraine." He kissed the side of her neck.

She turned towards him, placed a hand on his chest. "Nick, honey, you can't love me. I'm not right for you."

He laughed. "Not right for me? That's crazy."

"No, it's not," she whispered.

"Yes, it is."

She rolled onto her back, staring at the ceiling. "You don't know."

"Lorraine..."

She cut him off with a shake of her head. Then she told him about her married ex-lover with a son as old as Nick. She'd met him at the air conditioning and heating company, where he was lead technician and she was a part time secretary while attending community college.

"It just happened," she said, drawing the covers up to her shoulders. "I saw him around the office. He was one of the more mature guys, you know, not staring all the time like some of the younger ones."

Nick blushed slightly, but she seemed not to notice. "I mean, I knew he was checking me out, he is a guy, but he was just very cool, sweet even." She paused, her expression softened by the flicker of a smile Nick knew was not for him. "Anyway, we'd talk and some-times he'd buy me a cup of coffee. And a couple of times he gave me a ride home when my car was in the shop. He told me about his wife, his family. I mean, he never lied about that or tried to hide it. And then one night he made a move, and the next thing you know we're checking into the Days Inn." She looked at him. "Now do you see? You deserve better."

Nick shook his head. *You deserve better*, he wanted to tell her. Better than some middle-aged married guy. He felt a rush of ten-derness, a desire to protect her.

"Of course, I knew for him it was just sex," she said. "I'm not stupid. The thing is I really didn't care." She said she knew it couldn't last, but what was funny, what she hadn't expected, was that Petrocelli changed. He grew more serious, described his life as constricted, his marriage an old habit. He wanted something more, and Lorraine started to believe she could be the something more.

She stopped, her eyes filling with tears. Nick pulled her close, felt her cheek against his chest. He stroked her hair, uncertain what to say and acutely aware of his arousal.

"It's all right," she whispered, lifting her face to kiss him. He didn't know whether she was talking to him or to herself, and a

6

moment later he didn't care.

• • •

In the emergency room, Nick sat between Lorraine and Petrocelli, holding a clipboard of medical forms and a pen the woman behind the reception counter had given him.

"Here," Lorraine said, taking the clipboard. "Let me do that for you."

Nick had left the bloody washcloth in the car. He carefully touched his nose with his thumb and index finger, trying to gauge the damage.

"Careful," Lorraine said without looking up from the forms. "You'll make it start bleeding again."

Petrocelli smiled faintly, glancing at Nick before returning to the *Time* magazine he was paging through.

"Anything interesting?" Nick asked him.

"Same shit show as always."

Nick watched him turn the pages and noticed his thick fingers and wide hands. He wondered if they should be registered, like he'd heard as a kid that karate black belts were required to do. He felt his nose twinge. His father had strong, beefy hands, unlike Nick, whose long, slender fingers were more like his mother's.

"You keep up with world events and stuff?"

"I pay attention." Petrocelli didn't look up.

Nick nodded and folded his arms across his chest, hands tucked under his armpits. "Because you know Lorraine is really interested in the world. She's very intelligent."

Petrocelli smiled. "Oh, I know. Believe me." He jutted his chin towards Nick. "How's the nose?"

Nick felt his face start to flush. "Fine."

"You don't have any of these diseases or conditions, do you?"

7

Lorraine asked him, holding up the clipboard so he could read the list.

Nick glanced at the page, shook his head. "No."

"I didn't think so." She returned to the form, making neat checkmarks in the "No" column next to all the diseases and conditions. When she finished and Nick had signed, Lorraine looked at both of them.

"I'm going to take this up and go to the little girl's room. Can I leave you two alone?"

After she left, Nick looked at Petrocelli, who had gone back to reading his magazine.

"Can I ask you something?"

Petrocelli nodded.

"Do you love her?" Nick studied the older man's face for signs that the question caught him off guard, a sucker punch to expose the glass jaw of his true intentions.

Petrocelli regarded him for a moment. "Not that it's any of your business, but yes."

"Well that's good," Nick said, nodding slowly to protect his nose, his cheeks starting to flush again. He sat up straight, back pressed against the chair, drawing a steadying breath as he tried to match Petrocelli's calm demeanor. "That's good. Because she's not just somebody to fuck, you know."

Petrocelli closed the magazine and tossed it onto the low, square table in front of them. He leaned towards Nick, resting his thick arms on his knees, hands folded, his voice, when he spoke, a coarse sandpaper whisper.

"I left my wife and kids for Lorraine. You think that was easy? I changed my life for her. So, let me ask you. What have you done for her besides get your nose busted? Because you're right, she's not just somebody to fuck."

● ● ●

The morning after she told him about Petrocelli, Lorraine finished the story while she sat across from Nick at a window table of a storefront cafe, drinking coffee and sharing an order of toast. She said she could not continue being the other woman. Rumors had started. Around the office, looks were exchanged and conversations cut short when she entered the break room.

"No one ever said anything, but I knew from the way they looked." She was resting her chin in her hands, elbows on the table. "It was like I had my own scarlet letter, you know? Except mine would be H for homewrecker, or maybe S for slut." She quit her job in December and transferred to the university for the second semester. "I needed to get away," she said. "Clean break."

Nick sipped his coffee, carefully placing the cup back in the saucer before he looked at Lorraine. "So that's what you did, right? Made a clean break?"

"He's been calling me," she said.

"When?"

She looked down, ran her finger around the lip of her coffee cup. "Every day." She looked at Nick. "I'm sorry."

Nick took another sip of his coffee, trying to appear steady. He felt his head start to throb. "Is he going to leave his wife?"

She replied in a near whisper that he already had.

They sat silently. Sunlight emerged from behind a cloud and streamed through the window, bleaching the fading red and white check tablecloth. Patches of butter soaked into their slices of toast.

He squinted at her, eyes watery from the sunlight and the headache he'd had since waking up. "He doesn't love you."

A moment later she stood and when he started to do so, she put a hand on his shoulder. "Don't."

"What about last night? What was that?"

She touched his cheek, smiled and left. He watched her pass by the window, hands thrust into the pockets of her jeans, shoulders rolled forward, head slightly bowed. He thought she might steal a glance his way. He imagined their eyes locking through the glass and her face breaking into that lopsided smile, eyes filling with tears as she turned back towards the cafe's entrance. But she kept walking.

• • •

Nick and Petrocelli were sitting in silence when Lorraine returned. She squeezed Petrocelli's hand before she took her seat.

Petrocelli smiled at her, leaned back and slipped an arm around her shoulder before turning again to Nick. "I have to ask you something."

Nick nodded. "Okay."

"What exactly were you trying to do back at Tully's?"

It wasn't a taunt. There was a tone of genuine puzzlement in Petrocelli's gravelly voice. Nick shook his head as he realized none of his answers would make sense. The day after Lorraine left him sitting in the cafe, Nick borrowed his roommate's car and headed towards Howard, the town Lorraine was from. He opened the driver's side window all the way, allowing the air to slap his face in uneven bursts while the whirr and whine drowned his thoughts. He didn't call or text, which she could ignore. He would find her and tell her she was wrong, convince her she was making a mistake. He would rescue her from herself.

An hour after he left campus he drove down the main street of Howard. He pulled into a Shell gas station to use the men's room and then went inside and asked the clerk behind the counter if he had a local phone book.

"Over there." He pointed to a pay phone in the corner.

Nick nodded and went to the pay phone. He didn't know Lorraine's address and nothing had come up on Google. Her last name was Swanson. He opened the phone book to the S's and ran his finger down the pages until he found Swanson. There were four listings. How could there be four Swansons in a dinky little town like Howard? He checked that the clerk wasn't watching before tearing the page from the book, folding it and stuffing it into his back pocket. He slid the book back into the small shelf under the phone and returned to the counter.

"Is there a good place to get breakfast?"

"Tully's. Two blocks down on the right." The clerk pointed toward the street.

At Tully's he sat at the counter and ordered bacon, eggs and coffee. While waiting for his order he stared at the listings for Swanson on the phone book page as if they were a secret code, the unlocking of which would tell him what to do next. He was still looking at them when he heard Lorraine's voice say, "Jesus." He turned and saw her standing in the entrance next to a middle-aged guy who looked like he'd played linebacker in high school and never gotten out of shape. Nick stood and walked over to them.

"What are you doing here?" Lorraine asked.

"I have to talk to you."

"No, you don't."

"Yes, I do. Please."

"This is nuts." She started to walk past him but he grabbed her shoulders.

"Lorraine, please."

She stepped backwards and Nick released his grip.

"Okay, that's enough," the man said.

"I'm not talking to you."

The man stepped in front of Lorraine. "You are now."

"No," Nick said. "I am not." He tried to get by but the man held his arms out. "Great." Then he looked at Lorraine. "I'm not fucking leaving until I talk to you."

The hostess, a heavy-set woman in red slacks and a billowy powder blue blouse that looked like a maternity top, asked if there was a problem.

"I just want to talk to this woman."

"Perhaps you'd better leave, sir," the hostess said.

"I haven't finished eating."

"Then perhaps you should finish your breakfast."

"Five minutes, Lorraine. Please."

Over the man's shoulder Nick saw Lorraine close her eyes and nod. She touched the man's arm. "It's okay."

Turning to her, the man asked, "Are you sure?"

Loraine touched the side of his face and smiled. "Yes."

Outside Tully's, Nick told Lorraine that he loved her. Leaning into her so that her face filled his vision like a close-up in a movie, he asked in a low pleading voice how could she quit school? How could she throw everything away?

"What am I throwing away?"

"Everything. Your future. Your life."

Lorraine smiled. "Nick, sweetie, this is my life."

"Like hell it is."

The man, Petrocelli, had been standing off to the side. He stepped closer. "Okay, son, you've had your say."

"I'm not your son." Nick turned to face him, voice rising.

"C'mon, Lorraine." Petrocelli reached for her hand.

"Fuck you!" Nick shoved Petrocelli.

"Take it easy, son."

Nick swung at him—a wild punch that nearly struck Lorraine and grazed Petrocelli's chin. He started to swing again when he saw a flash of something coming at his face and felt the side of his nose crack. He started to topple backwards, caught his balance and bent over, grabbing his nose with one hand and holding the other up in the direction of Petrocelli. For a moment, the pain was so disorienting he was grateful not to have thrown up or passed out.

• • •

When they drove him back to his car, Lorraine asked if he was sure he was okay to drive.

Nick nodded. At the hospital, they had stuffed cotton up each nostril, taped a plastic splint to his nose and given him Tylenol. He looked at her standing next to Petrocelli, her arm slipped around his waist, his draped across her shoulders. "I better go," he said.

He took his time driving back. He kept the window rolled up and allowed his mind to drift as he watched the flat Illinois countryside roll by. He thought of Lorraine and Petrocelli as he had left them, holding each other, as if they had always been together. The car felt small and cramped and the road longer than it had that morning. He gripped the wheel and cursed to fight back the urge to cry. He knew crying would really fuck his nose up.

Nick's roommate tried to cheer him up by saying well-intentioned but stupid things like: "You had to know it wasn't going to last forever," and "There's a lot of pussy in the pond." He invited Nick to go with him to parties and told him he should work the busted nose while he could, but Nick declined.

He started to take walks at night, not through campus, but along the nearby residential streets lined with houses and apartments students rented. He avoided the street Lorraine had lived on until one night a week before finals. The evening he drove back from Howard he called to let her know he had arrived safely. She thanked him for letting him know and told him to take care. That was the last he'd heard from her. Now, a month later, he stopped and looked up at the dark window of her old apartment on the second floor. He'd been trying to think of her less to avoid memories that buckled him with desire. Standing on the empty street at close to midnight, the memories seemed slightly surreal. He wondered what their time together had meant to Lorraine. He wondered if it had meant anything at all.

"I know what you love," she had said, "and it isn't me." But now he realized it was Lorraine who knew what she loved, and it wasn't him.

Knowing

Few people came to Brenda's house after the funeral, and most didn't stay long. By nine o'clock only Janet remained. She and Brenda sat at the kitchen table sharing a pack of cigarettes and a second bottle of white wine, which one of them stood to retrieve from the refrigerator whenever their glasses were low.

"Why would she say that? I mean, Jesus, why say something like that?" Brenda tapped her cigarette against the side of a cut-glass ashtray the color of ginger ale.

"Did she say it to you?" Janet asked.

Brenda shook her head. "No, I was going outside to smoke and I heard her talking to some people from work. 'What an angry way to die.' Like she's some kind of goddamn suicide expert."

"Well, that's just Pam, you know, she always has to have something to say."

Brenda nodded and exhaled, the smoke curled up towards the three-pronged overhead fixture casting harsh light onto the laminate tabletop. The house was otherwise dark except for the front porch light, which Rick switched on before he went to bed. He had been sitting with them earlier, drinking beer, his eyes shifting from one to the other as if he were watching their conversation as much as listening to it. Without a word, he'd slid out of his chair, bent on one knee and wrapped Brenda in his arms, mashing her head against his chest. Then he kissed her on the forehead. His red-rimmed eyes glistened in the stark light.

"Try to sleep," Brenda told him.

"How's he doing?" Janet asked after he'd disappeared into the darkened house.

"He blames himself."

Janet nodded and sipped her wine. She traced her finger along a hairline scratch on the table.

"What?" Brenda asked.

Janet looked at her. "I was just thinking how he must feel."

"It wasn't his fault."

"I know," Janet said.

"But it was his gun." Brenda shook her head. "That's what you're thinking, isn't it? That's what everybody's thinking, right?"

"I don't know what everybody's thinking."

"But here's the thing, Janet. Here's the thing," Brenda smiled like someone with the answer to a riddle. "I'm the one who let him bring it into the house."

The gun was from the time Rick did long haul driving. He'd often slept in the cab of his truck and having the pistol made him feel safer. That's what he told Brenda. He was off the road by the time they met seven years ago, an assistant manager in an auto parts store, but he'd kept the gun. He told her he was used to having it. Brenda loved the deep calm of his voice, the strength of his hand cupping her shoulder when he put his arm around her, and the gentle way he played with Melanie. When he said he would keep it in a locked metal box on the top shelf in the bedroom closet, Brenda agreed the gun could stay.

The police said Melanie must have found the key to the metal box in the back of the top dresser drawer where Rick hid it under balled pairs of socks. She knew about the metal box and the gun because Rick showed her when she turned thirteen.

"She needs to know it's not a toy," he said to Brenda. "She's old enough to understand. I'd rather show her than have her come across it by accident." He spoke in the calm and measured way he had, the way that made her feel safe.

Brenda and Janet sat at the kitchen table past midnight, until Brenda suddenly felt the weight of the day and the wine. When she thought again of stepping onto the wide, wraparound porch of the funeral home and overhearing Pam, grief rose in her like nausea. It was an angry way to die.

• • •

"I missed something," Brenda said to Rick. They were sitting on lawn chairs in the backyard, where Rick had coaxed her to come after he found her curled on Melanie's bed when he got home from work. She looked straight ahead as she spoke, staring at the pink and blue hues of the sunset. Rick sipped his beer.

"I don't know what. But there had to be something."

She felt Rick's hand on her thigh and turned to him.

"You shouldn't blame yourself," he said. He was tall and round-shouldered, with an angular face and hazel eyes that blinked as he leaned closer. "You did the best you could with her."

"Not good enough." She felt her eyes sting and looked away, taking a sip of her iced tea. When she looked at him again she gripped his hand. "Sorry."

"No need."

"I just feel like there has to be a reason. There does, doesn't there?"

Rick shook his head. "I don't know. I guess." He sat back in his chair, gently withdrawing his hand from hers and rubbing his eyes. "One thing I learned from all those years on the road is life can be fucked up."

"What do you mean, like it just happened? Some random act?"

"No, no," he said, the pitch of his voice rising. "Just that bad things sometimes happen."

Brenda wanted the deep calm to return to his voice. She wished they were on the sofa so she could lean into him and be held. She smiled and rubbed his arm as he slouched in his chair, head tilted back to look at the first evening stars.

"My mother wanted me to give Melanie up for adoption, did I ever tell you that?"

Rick shook his head. Brenda sat back in her chair. Across the street that flanked the backyard was a small municipal park. There wasn't much to it: a couple of swing sets, monkey bars, and a slide, an open field with the metal frame of soccer goals on each end. But it was a place to play and one of the reasons she rented the house. She'd taken Melanie there on spring and summer evenings when there was still light after she got home from work, and on Saturday mornings when she'd bring a mug of coffee and sit on the bench next to the swings. She'd watched Melanie lean back in the swing and pump her legs the way Brenda had taught her, propelling herself forward and back, hair streaming behind her, smiling as she picked up speed, lifting higher, glancing at Brenda to be sure she was watching.

"Maybe I should have. Maybe she'd be alive if I had."

"Don't say that."

Brenda shrugged. "Who knows? She might have done better in a normal family."

Rick sat up.

"I'm sorry," Brenda said, "I didn't mean... I was just thinking about all the time before we met."

Rick took a long pull of beer. "I loved her too, you know."

Melanie had not been a deal-breaker for Rick, like she had

been for most men Brenda dated. He said family was important to him. His parents were farmers in southwest Missouri, and as he put it, "bat-shit crazy Bible-thumpers." As an only child, his life was restricted to school, chores, and church. He left right after high school, eventually becoming a trucker, a job that fit his restless nature, his need to move and breathe. He worried his upbringing had taught him little about being a father. Still, he told her the idea appealed to him, the chance to do it the right way.

Brenda set her glass on the ground and held his hand in both of hers. "I'm sorry," she whispered. "Everything feels so crazy. I just want to know why."

He nodded, freed his hand, went into the house.

• • •

When she woke the next morning, Brenda knew she had to move. She lay thinking of all they would have to do. Give notice to the landlord, find a new place, sort through everything, pack. Then she thought: *Melanie's ashes*. She closed her eyes and took a deep breath, then another, hands folded across her chest like a carved figure on a coffin.

Rick was sitting at the kitchen table drinking coffee. She kissed the top of his head before pouring herself a mug and sitting across from him.

"We have to move."

He looked at her.

She braced her arms on the table and held her coffee mug with both hands. "I can't live here anymore."

"This house?"

"Yes."

He nodded slowly, eyes cast downward. "We can do whatever you want, you know that. But I've heard it's not a good idea to make changes right after something like this, that it's better to wait a bit."

"How long?"

"I don't know. It's just what I've heard."

She started to cry. He brought his chair around next to hers and held her.

"We can move whenever you want," he said. "It doesn't matter to me."

"Rick," she said after a moment. "We might have to leave Sangamon. I don't know if I can stay this close."

They stayed through the summer, three months when Brenda felt like she was watching her life being lived. She was aware of going through each day, of seeing people at work and the grocery store and in her neighborhood. She heard herself speaking, but conversations had become collections of sounds. She and Rick spread a map of the United States on the kitchen table and looked at cities, measuring distances. Sangamon was in central Illinois which meant they could get far away going east or west. Eventually, they decided on Phoenix, and Rick set about finding a job there.

Each day Brenda walked to the end of the hallway to Melanie's bedroom. A stuffed elephant, faded and gray, leaned against the pillow of the neatly made bed, its black cloth eye staring at Brenda. A shelf along one wall was nearly empty except for yearbooks from middle school and high school, the first three "Harry Potter" novels, and all of the "Twilight" series. The wall opposite the book shelf was freshly painted. Some days Brenda stared at it, watching the movement of light speckled through lace curtains, until in her mind's eye she saw again the dark stain, a Rorschach splattering.

"Jesus, Melanie," she'd whisper.

• • •

Brenda was nineteen when she discovered she was pregnant with Melanie. She wasn't sure who the father was.

"There are many couples in need," her mother said. "They can give the baby a good life."

"I can give the baby a good life."

Her mother shook her head. "Not as good as a married couple."

They were in the living room of her parents' house, seated on opposite ends of a faded turquoise sofa. The draperies were open but the front windows admitted scant light in late afternoon. Her mother picked at a bit of thread on one of the slip covers. "It's not easy raising a child alone."

It was a reference to Brenda's father. She remembered him sitting on the same sofa, sipping his scotch and watching golf or football. Sometimes he'd just stare out the front window, as if waiting for something to pass by. One Sunday afternoon when Brenda was a high school freshman, he stood during a commercial break of a Bears-Packers game, started to cross the room, and dropped dead of a cerebral hemorrhage.

"Your father could be difficult," Brenda's mother continued, still not looking up. "I can say that to you now that you're grown. Half the time I didn't know where his mind was. But whatever his faults, he was a good provider."

"I know."

Brenda took a job as a secretary at a local insurance brokerage and, when she advanced to office manager, she moved to the small rambler. Melanie was three. The first night in the house she tucked Melanie in, poured a glass of wine, and walked through all the rooms. She settled onto the sofa in the living room. Stillness permeated the house. There were no passing cars, no sounds coming from the neighbors' homes. She set her empty glass on the coffee table, buried her face in her hands and wept. *We can be happy here,* she thought.

It was just the two of them and Brenda worried their solitude was turning Melanie inward. She did well enough in school, she had friends, but she always seemed to be on the periphery. Brenda's mother said she was just quiet, like Brenda's father. She watched Melanie while Brenda worked, and on the Saturday nights Brenda had a date or went out with her girlfriends. Brenda felt odd coming home to her own house and being met by her mother, as if she were still in high school.

"What?" she asked one time, slumping onto the sofa, watching her mother gather her purse and the cloth bag containing her needlepoint.

"You need to be careful."

"Jesus, Mom, I have to have a life."

"You have a daughter. You can't be out drinking and whatnot until all hours."

"Whatnot?" Brenda giggled.

"You know what I mean."

Brenda nodded, closing her eyes and resting her head against the sofa. "Oh, I do know what you mean. But don't worry, Mom, there's not a lot of whatnot going on around here lately."

"Lately."

Brenda opened her eyes. She was fuzzy-headed with wine and too tired to argue, not that it would make any difference. Her mother saw only mistakes.

• • •

Since the funeral Janet stopped by a couple of evenings a week, and on Fridays she brought a pizza and a bottle of wine. Rick took a couple of slices and a beer into the living room to watch the Cardinals, leaving Janet and Brenda at the kitchen table.

"I think she was happy here," Brenda said. "You know?"

Janet nodded and smiled at Brenda. "Of course she was. She was a good girl, we all know that."

"And beautiful." Brenda fished a cigarette from the pack on the table. Melanie had luxurious raven hair and pale green eyes. She had always seemed unaware of her beauty and the power it gave her, part of her quiet nature, Brenda thought. Rick had helped to draw her out. Melanie was eight when he moved into the rambler. He crossed his eyes and twisted his long face into silly contortions, tousled her hair, took her to the park to kick a soccer ball or play catch. When he slouched on the sofa, stretching his legs onto the coffee table, Melanie sat on his lap and rested her head against his long chest, giggling at the deep rumbling sound his voice made.

Brenda lit her cigarette and looked across the table at her friend. "Can I ask you something personal?"

"Of course."

"Do you ever pray?"

Janet shrugged. "Sometimes. I think everybody does sometimes, right?"

"The only time I pray," Brenda said, "is when I need something. Do you think that means my prayers aren't as good as people who pray all the time?"

"I don't know, honey. I never thought about it that way."

"My mom used to pray all the time. I think she prayed for me. I know she prayed for Melanie." Brenda exhaled, tapping the end of the cigarette on the lip of the ashtray. "Probably prayed to save her from me." She smiled without parting her lips, eyes cast downward. Her mother had been a devout Catholic who saw no humor in Brenda describing herself as a "recovering" Catholic. "She told me I should have Melanie baptized. She used to be on me all the time about that after Melanie was born. But I couldn't do that,

Janet. You know? I mean I didn't want to be a hypocrite. I'm not sure I believe any of that crap, not really."

Janet nodded.

"But now I think, could it have made Melanie happy? Maybe given her something?"

"Oh, honey, you gave her everything you could. You were a good mother."

"You really think so?"

"Oh my God, yes," Janet replied. She blinked back tears and shook her head. "I'm sorry." She waved her hand in front of her face as if trying to cool it. "I'm sorry," she repeated. "It just makes me so sad."

For some reason, Brenda thought of their eighth-grade soccer team. During team huddles, just before the game started, all the players piled their hands one on top of the other while the coach made a little speech that always ended with something corny like, "Win on three. One-two-three, win!"

"Life sucks on three," Brenda said, a hoarse laugh bursting out of her. "Remember that?"

Janet was startled but covered it with a smile as she watched Brenda laugh, then cough, then stare across the table, gripping Janet's hand.

"Do you really think I was a good mother, Janet? You aren't just saying that?"

• • •

One evening in late July, Brenda asked Rick if they should have married. They were sitting in the backyard watching neighborhood kids playing soccer in the park.

"Do you want to get married?" Rick shifted in his seat, took a sip of beer.

"It doesn't matter now. I was thinking about Melanie."

Rick shook his head, stared at the label on his beer bottle.

"I'm not finding fault," Brenda said. "I know you were good to her. I know that." Melanie had never resisted Rick like she did Brenda. He had a way of coaxing her out of her bad moods, slyly teasing her until she laughed. He always tried to build her up, told her how beautiful she was, even during this past year, when she was more and more sullen. He wasn't afraid to show his emotions, like a lot of men. Janet called him a hugger, rolling her eyes. Brenda remembered how he pulled Melanie into bear hugs, and put an arm around her shoulder when they walked over to the park to kick the soccer ball or sit on the swings and talk. They were as close as any father and daughter could be.

"I just keep thinking about what I could have done different."

"Well maybe," Rick turned to her. "You're thinking too much. Maybe there isn't an answer." He spoke in the calm voice that had always reassured Brenda, brow furrowed, but she could see in his eyes the struggle to mask his irritation.

"Maybe," she said. "But I can't help it."

"It's your mother. She's still in your head, from beyond the grave." He took a long pull of beer.

"I can't help that either."

Her mother thought it was a mistake to allow Rick to move in unless a ring was involved. She said it was a bad example to set for Melanie and dismissed Brenda's argument that Rick was really good with her.

"He's a charmer," her mother had said. "Charm is easy."

"He's like a father to Melanie."

"Except he's not."

Brenda had little patience with her mother's fault-finding. She spoke to her less and considered other ways of cutting her off, such as restricting the time she spent with Melanie. Ways to say the three of them—Rick, Brenda, and Melanie—were a family and didn't need her mother or her approval. Rick talked her out of it, saying she'd regret it after her mother was gone. Now she was, along with Melanie, leaving Brenda to make sense of it.

• • •

All summer Brenda tried to recall when Melanie started to slip away.

She was a good girl. Not perfect. Sometimes Brenda had to get on her. Once when she was fourteen she emerged from the bathroom wrapped in a towel to cross the hall to her bedroom. Brenda told her she wasn't a child anymore, she needed to wear a robe. Melanie rolled her eyes and mumbled "Whatever." Other times she had a smart mouth, but Brenda had a smart mouth when she was that age. She thought all kids did.

During the last year, something changed. Melanie was gone more and when she was home, she was moodier. Sometimes even Rick couldn't draw her out. From the kitchen window Brenda watched them walk to the park after dinner one evening and sit side by side on the park bench. She could see Rick talking, gesturing, draping an arm across Melanie's shoulders, while Melanie seemed to do little more than stare at the ground.

"I was trying to make her understand she doesn't have it so bad around here," he'd said when Brenda asked what they had been talking about. "Not like the shit box I grew up in."

"Did you say that?"

"No, of course not. But I did tell her she was lucky to have parents who loved her and cared what happened to her."

"What did she say?"

"You're not my father."

"What?"

"She said, 'You're not my father.'"

Brenda shook her head. "Jesus Christ."

"Yeah, something's going on with her, but I'll be goddamned if I know what it is."

Brenda blamed Melanie's boyfriend, Derek, with his skinny, slouching posture and sullen, pimply face. She hated the dead-eyed, possessive looks he cast towards Melanie. Worse was the way Melanie leaned into him, allowing herself to be held, anxious to please.

"I don't like what he's doing to you." Brenda said one night. She'd fallen asleep on the sofa watching the news and was awakened when Melanie pushed open the front door.

Melanie laughed.

"What's funny?"

"All this concern about my well-being."

"What?"

"Nothing. Kidding"

Brenda stared at her for a moment. "Can you sit down?"

Melanie crossed to the sofa and dropped to a sitting position.

"Are you okay?"

"Suuure." Melanie's voice seemed to come from the edge of a dream.

"Are you high?"

"Are you?" Melanie nodded towards the wine glass on the coffee table.

"I'm worried about you, honey."

"Why?"

"Because of what he's doing to you, the way he's changing you."

"Who?"

"You know who. Derek."

Melanie leaned forward, a smile etching across her mouth, eyes unfocused. "What do you think he's doing, fucking me?"

Brenda slapped her. The sound was startling, as if disconnected from her action. A red mark welled on the side of Melanie's cheek. "Oh God, I'm sorry."

Melanie leaned back, fingering the side of her face. "Don't worry, he's not fucking me."

Brenda tried to control the tremble in her voice. "I'm sorry. I just want you to be happy."

Melanie laughed, head bobbing forward and back as if it were suddenly too heavy for her neck to support. "Is that all? Okay, Mommy. I'm happy."

When Brenda told Rick, he frowned. "What exactly did she say?"

"That she wasn't having sex with that little shit. She said, 'Don't worry, he's not fucking me.' But in a really sarcastic, smart ass way." Brenda drew a cigarette from her pack. Rick nodded while he fished a lighter from his shirt pocket and lit her cigarette.

"That's how kids are these days. It's all about shock value, seeing how far they can push it."

Brenda exhaled. "I worry that I'm losing her."

"You're not losing her."

"I think about those girls at the truck stops."

When they first met, Rick told her about life on the road, including the teenage girls. Runaways. He knew what would happen to most of them, saw them walking in the shadows between the rigs, and it made him sick. He started to talk to some of them, asked where they were from and why they were on the road. Sometimes he offered them bus fare home, other times he gave them rides, figuring, he said, they were safer with him than the predators he saw eye-balling them.

"Melanie's a good girl, she'll be all right."

She nodded, wanting to believe his assurance.

"I'll tell you what," Rick said, leaning back in his chair, "pretty as Melanie is I don't know what she sees in that little jerk." He shook his head and smiled, but behind it Brenda saw a trace of hurt, even anger.

• • •

As the summer wore on, Brenda began to realize she could never get far enough away, and although she'd said nothing to Rick, she had started to think she needed to be on her own. It was an instinct at first, like a craving for a particular food which her mother always said was the body's way of saying it needed a certain nutrient. Brenda needed solitude. She'd find Rick standing in the doorway to Melanie's room, and when he turned to her there was more than sadness in his expression, more than guilt for having kept the gun. There was something beyond reach or comfort, and it unnerved her.

"Sorry," he'd say, pulling her into a hug. "I'm so sorry."

"It's okay," she'd answer. "I allowed it."

Then he'd kiss her forehead and wander off to watch a game on television or sit in his lawn chair in the backyard and sip a beer.

Later, if he reached to her side of the bed, his touch was needy, desperate. She'd keep her eyes open as he moved atop her, the darkness of the room an endless void, his breath gasping in her ear like a man climbing a steep hill. She'd pull him closer until she felt his shuddering halt. She wanted to be held, the reassuring calm of his voice, but when his breathing dissolved into a soft snore, she'd curl onto her side of the bed. Fear seized her like a hand at the back of the neck. She realized the fear was not new, but something uncovered, a light peeling away shadows. She'd close her eyes and pray "Dear God please help me" again and again, until the words numbed her into sleep.

• • •

On her last day in the house, Brenda sat at the kitchen table and thought about pouring a glass of wine from the bottle she had chilling in the refrigerator. But that was for after, she would need it to sleep. She tapped a cigarette from the pack on the table, lit it, and stared at the cardboard box sitting behind her ashtray and coffee mug.

Earlier that week, she'd told Rick she needed to be alone for a while. He should go on to Phoenix and start his new job.

"The job can wait."

She shook her head. "I just don't think I can be around anyone right now. I know that sounds strange."

He smiled tentatively, eyes narrowing. "Is there something you want to tell me?"

She looked at him. The creases in his face reminded her of the lines on maps marking rivers and streams. "I just need time."

Rick blinked several times, as if the effort of meeting her stare caused his eyes to sting. "Are you leaving me?"

"No," she said, not sure if it was true, which meant it might not be a lie.

"Shit. I knew it."

"Rick."

"That goddamn gun." He shook his head. "How many times do I have to say I'm sorry?"

"It's not the gun."

"Then what?" His expression wasn't sorrowful as it had been so often that summer, but hurt, angry, like a man falsely accused.

"Time," she said. "I just need time to myself."

She could tell he wanted to say more. She saw in the downward shift of his eyes a calculation, a weighing of words, but he remained silent. In the end, he did as she asked, loaded his tools and a duffel bag into the back of his truck and headed west.

It was four o'clock and time to go. Time while the cemetery gate was still open and there was sunlight. Brenda made sure her cigarette was out and rinsed the coffee mug in the sink. Turning to the table she exhaled audibly to suppress a shiver.

• • •

There were no other cars in sight when she drove through the gate of St. Luke's Catholic Cemetery. Late afternoon sunlight streaked through oaks and maples as she followed the narrow road up and around to the top of a small rise, where she slowed to a stop and parked. The branches of a maple cast dancing shadows on the hood of her car. Past the maple were the graves of nearly all the family members on her mother's side, starting with Brenda's great grandparents. Brenda had not been here since her mother's burial a little over a year earlier. Melanie had stood next to her that day, holding her hand as the priest recited the prayers of the Catholic burial service. Her daughter stared solemnly at the casket, her expression never changing. A presence but not present.

She opened the car door, took the cardboard box from the passenger side, and stepped out. The air brushed her face as she looked at the cluster of tombstones. Cradling the box against her chest with both arms, she walked across the grass to her parents' graves. Behind them were her grandparents and great grandparents and to each side various aunts and uncles, and one cousin killed in a head on collision when he was sixteen and Brenda was seven.

She knelt and gently placed the box in front of her. The grass felt soft and cool through the knees of her slacks. She leaned all the way over and kissed the top of the box. "My sweet girl." She removed the lid and the black plastic bag and turned it upside down over her mother's grave, spilling a gray pile of ash and grit. On her hands and knees, she began to spread the pile, working it into the grass, lifting handfuls and casting them gently up and down and side to side as evenly as she could.

She sat back, eyes closed, hands upturned in her lap. She saw Melanie as she had discovered her—head against the wall, arms splayed, one leg tucked awkwardly under the other, like a ballerina who suddenly collapsed. The wall still wet and red with blood and brain. Brenda did not remember what happened after that. The police found her kneeling with Melanie's head in her lap, stroking the side of her face, rocking gently as if her daughter were sleeping.

Brenda opened her eyes. She rubbed her hands together, feeling the grit like grains of sand, then wiped them on the grass.

She prayed for God to forgive her. She lay on her side, the tombstones looming large and cold as she looked across the ash-strewn grass. She had decided to go to Florida. She'd call Rick when she got there. Could she tell him then? Explain the slow dread that had seeped into her that summer, like the fear of a terminal illness? Admit she had stayed hoping to find out it wasn't true?

Brenda closed her eyes and thought about the ocean, the utter silence beneath the warm, heavy water. She imagined it as a kind of baptism, a washing away of what she feared most: knowing.

A Place To Be

His brother's grave was in the northwest corner of the cemetery and after they'd finished loading the equipment, Randy paid his respects. That's how he described it to Doug, "pay my respects." Doug stayed with the pick-up truck, while Randy crossed to the far corner and stood in front of Ted's grave. He didn't say a prayer or speak to Ted, he just stared at the gray headstone and its inscription: *Theodore "Ted" Franklin / Lance Corporal USMC / June 14,1992-May 23, 2012*. Ted had been laid to rest six years ago, when Randy was twelve. There was an honor guard—two Marines—one of whom gave Randy's mother a folded flag. A bugler played Taps. A week before the funeral his mother had taken him to the JC Penney in Chesterton, the next town over, and bought him a black suit and tie and a white dress shirt. The sleeves of the suit clung to his arms in the heat and the shirt collar scratched his neck, but he didn't complain, nor cry. He watched the casket being lowered into the ground and thought how it would piss Ted off to end up here, less than a mile from where he grew up. Ted had joined the Marines to get out of Millwood, Illinois and the Marines had sent him back.

Randy looked up from the headstone to the fence ten yards away and the cornfield on the other side. A late afternoon breeze cooled the sweat under his T-shirt and filled his nostrils with the smell of fresh mown grass. He came here each time he and

Doug mowed the grounds of St. Paul's and the adjoining cemetery because it felt like the right thing to do. But he always ended up staring across the cornfield towards the flat horizon. He didn't believe in prayer and didn't know what to say.

He walked back to the truck, where Doug was sitting sideways in the driver's seat, feet propped on the running board, smoking a cigarette and sipping from a sixteen-ounce bottle of Mountain Dew.

"That shit will kill you," Randy said.

"Which?" Doug held up both hands, Mountain Dew in one, cigarette in the other, a smile spreading across his beefy face.

"Both."

"Everybody dies." Doug nodded towards the cemetery. "In case you hadn't noticed."

Randy smiled and went around to the passenger side.

They cut grass from April to November for St. Paul's, two businesses in town, and half a dozen residents. Doug called it lawn maintenance and talked about starting a landscaping business. Randy saved almost every dollar he earned. A landscaping business meant staying in Millwood and he wanted out as much as Ted had. He was headed to college in the fall.

Doug eased his truck onto Main Street and down the hill to the intersection. The buildings lining both sides looked worn— two-story structures of brick, or wood with vinyl siding. Ted used to say the buildings looked as bored with Millwood as he was. He only said it when he and Randy were alone, never in front of their parents. As they passed through the second intersection, Randy saw his father's Ford Taurus in an angled parking space in front of a vinyl-sided building on the corner. The wood sign above the door said *Franklin Insurance / Home, Auto, Life.*

"What's up tonight, anything?" Doug asked.

"I don't know, hadn't thought about it."

"I'll probably go by the lake and see if anything is happening."

Randy nodded. If anything was happening at the lake, it would involve beer, probably weed, and the possibility of a hook-up. It would also involve the same people: high school kids, those who had just graduated in June, like him and Doug, and older kids– the ones home from college for the summer and the ones who had never left. Summer nights in Millwood.

After the third intersection the downtown gave way to a series of residential streets. A three stop-light town, as Ted used to say. Doug turned right onto Randy's street and pulled up in front of his house, midway down the block.

"Call me if you want to hang out later," he said.

Randy nodded. Doug pulled away from the curb, then swerved hard right and back left in a looping U-turn, giving Randy a thumbs-up as he went by.

• • •

He called hello to his mother as he passed from the mud room through the kitchen.

"Hi, sweetie," she said, turning from the kitchen sink. "How was your day?"

He shrugged. "Same old same old."

"And Doug?"

"Same old Doug."

By the time he'd showered and changed his father had come home. Randy found him sitting in the living room in his brown leather Barcalounger, sipping his nightly scotch and watching the news. He smiled as Randy took a seat on the sofa.

"How goes the lawn maintenance business?"

Randy smirked. "You sound like Doug."

"Nothing wrong with a little entrepreneurial spirit."

"This is Doug we're talking about."

His father shook his head, went back to watching the news. Randy thought if he left for ten years and came back on a weeknight at 6:00 PM, he'd find his father sitting in the same chair, sipping scotch, watching the news.

After the news, they took their places around the dining room table, his parents on each end, Randy in the middle. There was a chair opposite him, Ted's chair, tucked neatly in place. For the first year after he was killed, his mother set a place for him each evening, as if he were just late for dinner and would arrive at any moment. His father said it was an expression of grief, like laying flowers at the grave. Randy worried it was something more serious. But he grew accustomed to seeing the placemat and folded napkin, fork, knife, and spoon set opposite him until one evening the space was empty, the dark wood shiny and bare.

Now his father asked Randy how his day had been.

"Fine." Randy reached for the bowl of new potatoes and ladled several onto his plate where they settled next to two slices of ham.

"Good," his father said in the deliberately cheerful tone that Randy imagined him using with clients. "What did you do?"

Randy said he and Doug had taken care of the church grounds and the cemetery, mowing and pruning. The words rose out of him begrudgingly, as if the question had invaded some private space.

Ted always knew how to talk to their father, how to answer his questions without betraying the slightest hint of the annoyance Randy struggled to suppress. Ted made everything look easy. If he were there to ask how he did it, Randy knew Ted would just shrug. "It's not a big deal."

It's what he had said when he announced his intention to enlist. He did so over dinner, dropping it into the conversation as casually as he would plans for a weekend fishing trip.

"I've been talking to a recruiter."

"What?" Their father had set down his fork and rested his elbows on the table.

Their mother had stared at Ted. Her older brother had been drafted during Vietnam and killed three months after being deployed. Lingering sunlight from the dining room window fell across her face.

"There is no draft," she'd said. "You don't have to do this."

Ted shrugged and said he had to do something. When their mother flinched, absorbing his flippant reply like a slap across the face, he slid his chair to her end of the table and took her hand in his. "Mom, I'll be fine. It's not a big deal."

Now his father asked his mother about her day and told her about his, leaving Randy to finish his meal in silence. After dinner, he helped clear the table and load the dishwasher, then called Doug. Predictable.

• • •

"Let's skip the lake," Randy said as he got into the passenger side of Doug's truck.

"Seriously? Shit, I procured us a six-pack." By procure Doug meant stole from the ready supply his father kept in their garage refrigerator—from what Randy had observed, never less than a case, often closer to two.

"So? It'll keep. I'm not up for the lake."

"What do you want to do?" Doug asked.

"I don't know. Go over to Chesterton, or up to Sangamon."

"Sangamon? Dude, that's fifty miles."

"Let's just get on the road."

Doug shook his head as he turned onto Main Street. "You're

fuckin' weird sometimes, Franklin. You know that, don't you?"

"Just drive."

"Okay. Reach into the back and pop open one of those beers for me."

Randy frowned. "Really?"

"What? I have a cup holder."

They headed east on the state highway, a two-lane road running between fields of corn and soybeans. Randy opened a beer for Doug and got one for himself. He knew it was weird, but it felt good to be moving, to watch the fences and utility poles whiz by. He popped the tab.

The week before Ted shipped to Afghanistan, they had driven to Chesterton for a movie and dinner afterwards at Applebee's. Just the two of them. It was Ted's goodbye gift. He'd done something with each of them—taken their mother to dinner at her favorite restaurant in Sangamon, risen early on his last Saturday in Millwood to go fishing with their father. In Applebee's people who knew him stopped by their table to shake his hand and thank him for his service. Ted smiled and said he hadn't done anything yet. When Randy asked him if he was nervous about going to Afghanistan, Ted laughed and rested his arms on the table, looking at Randy across the clutter of empty plates and glasses.

"You've got to make your own luck. I didn't see that happening in Millwood."

"Yeah, Millwood sucks."

"Not for everyone," Ted replied, and when Randy frowned, added, "just for guys like us."

Randy wanted to ask him again if he was nervous, but Ted signaled for the check and the moment passed.

Now Doug lifted his beer. "Here's how we lost the farm." It was the same lame toast he made every time they drank. Randy figured he had heard it from his father who had heard it from his father, although neither one was a farmer. He touched his beer can to Doug's.

They slowed to pass through Chesterton, a town not much bigger than Millwood but with a small outdoor mall including a Target, a Home Depot, a Taco Bell, and a few local stores. Cars surrounded the Applebee's where he and Ted had eaten dinner, light and movement visible through the windows under the red awnings. The JC Penney where Randy got his suit for Ted's funeral was abandoned, ghostly, the doors and windows gaping black against the white facade.

"So, when are you leaving for college? Soon, right?"

Randy nodded. "Three weeks."

"Shit."

Randy looked at him. "You should have applied somewhere."

"I don't know."

"You totally could have gotten in somewhere if you'd applied."

Doug shook his head. "College is not my thing, okay?"

"But Millwood is?"

"Kind of. It's not so bad."

"Seriously?" Randy laughed.

"Yeah, dude. Seriously. Not everyone is as anxious to get out of Dodge as you."

Randy had known Doug since kindergarten. They'd been in the same classes, played Little League and high school baseball together, seen each other, Randy realized when he thought about it, almost every day of their lives since they were five years old. Yet he sometimes wondered how they had remained friends.

After they pulled onto the interstate, Doug asked for another beer.

Randy handed it to him. "Take it easy."

"Whatever."

The fields were further away and nearly invisible in the dark. In the distance lights from farmhouses and an occasional gas station punctuated the blackness.

"You really serious about starting a landscaping business?" Randy asked after a few minutes.

"Why not? I've got a lot of the equipment and some customers. I like working outside."

Randy nodded.

"The world's a pretty fucked up place right now, in case you hadn't noticed," Doug said. He took a long swallow of beer. "We've got illegals all over the damn place, ISIS bastards that want to kill us. Why do I want to get mixed up in all that crap if I can make a nice life for myself in Millwood?"

"And you think you can make a nice life for yourself in Millwood?"

"Yeah," Doug nodded. "Yeah I do." He glanced at Randy. "You think you can make a nice life somewhere else?"

Randy shrugged. "I guess I'll find out." He didn't have a plan beyond leaving for college, not even a half-assed one like Doug's. All he knew was he couldn't stay in Millwood. At Ted's funeral, Father Baker, who had been the parish priest at St. Paul's for as long as Randy could remember, said the death of such a young man was a great test of faith, but we must trust that God had a purpose and a plan for each of us. Randy wanted to believe that but couldn't. He was pretty sure Ted would have called bullshit too.

As they got closer to Sangamon, farmhouses and fields gave way to strip malls and office parks. Black and white speed limit signs read 45 and then 35, and a green sign marking the city limit read "Pop. 103,234." Ten times the size of Millwood. Randy had been to Sangamon with his parents and Ted for special occasions like Mother's Day or Easter brunch, or to visit the History Museum. His favorite exhibit was the diorama with carved figures behind plate glass depicting Native Americans around campfires and tee-pees, bears and buffalo, and the early pioneers with their covered wagons and horse-drawn ploughs. Ted thought it was lame, but Randy stood for long stretches in front of each window studying the figures: bare-chested Indian men, Indian women in buckskin shifts, their hair black and shoulder length, with headbands and feathers. The pioneer women wore long cotton dresses and white bonnets, the men dark cotton pants and loose, long sleeve shirts. The bodies were perfectly proportioned, posed at some task, unblinking expressions on the carved faces. Except for the lifeless eyes, they were like real people, frozen in time and space.

They drove to the downtown area, the older part of Sangamon, and around the courthouse square.

"Abe Lincoln argued cases in that courthouse." Randy pointed to the old sandstone building in the center of the square.

Doug snorted.

"Don't be a moron," Randy said.

"Don't be a fucking tour guide."

Randy lifted his left hand and extended his middle finger.

"Nice. Real nice. So now that you dragged us here, what do you want to do?"

Randy shrugged. "I don't know, man. I just felt like driving."

"You mean riding." Doug grinned at him, then said the first thing he had to do was take a piss.

"And maybe get some coffee."

Doug nodded. "Yeah, okay."

They stopped at an IHOP and were seated in a booth. The blonde Formica tabletop glowed yellow in the overhead light and smelled faintly of disinfectant. Doug ordered a short stack and a coffee. Their waiter was an Asian kid with a sprinkle of acne on his forehead who nodded the entire time he was writing their order. The restaurant wasn't crowded. Two couples who looked as old as Randy's parents were seated at a table, and three college-aged girls were seated at a booth along the adjacent wall. Doug lifted his chin in the direction of the girls and raised his eyebrows.

"You wish," Randy said.

The waiter brought Doug's order. Randy sipped his coffee and glanced at their reflection in the window: Doug bent over his plate, slicing his fork through the pancakes; Randy's own face pensive, staring back at him from out of the dark.

Doug dipped a forkful of pancake into a puddle of syrup. The door of the restaurant opened and two couples entered, the men wearing turbans and the women long head scarves. Doug looked up from his food and watched as the hostess seated them in a booth next to the college girls.

"Damn," Doug said softly.

"What?"

Doug screwed his face into a look of disbelief. "What do you think?"

"Seriously? C'mon, man. Chill."

"I'm fine. Just not used to eating in the same place as Muslims."

Randy shook his head. "Dude, they're not Muslims, they're Indians. From India. Sikhs."

Doug set his fork on his plate. "They look like Muslims."

"But they're not, I'm telling you. There have been stories about them getting shot because some crazy redneck thought they were Muslim."

"You calling me a crazy redneck?"

"I wouldn't call you crazy."

"Fuck you." Doug grinned and sat back, pushing his plate

away. He lifted his coffee mug and sipped while stealing glances at the Indian couples. After a moment he set his mug down and leaned across the table. "Doesn't it bother you at all?"

"What?"

"Just look around. Our waiter is some kind of Chinese guy, the hostess is black, one of those couples at the table is black, I bet all the help in the back are black or Mexican. And then you have the Muslims or Indians or whatever. I mean, I like people, but I don't know."

"It's the world."

Doug nodded. "You're welcome to it, college boy. I'll take Millwood."

• • •

Randy drove on the way back while Doug went to work on the remaining beers. He finished one soon after they were back on the interstate and popped open another.

"Take it easy," Randy said.

"What? You're driving, and besides, those pancakes gave my stomach a nice coating."

There was little traffic on the interstate. The road unspooled before the headlights in smooth, mesmerizing chunks, and Randy shifted his gaze to stay alert. Doug stared out the passenger window. They drove in silence until Doug chugged the last of his beer, crumpled the can and dropped it behind the seats. "Sometimes I miss Ted."

Randy nodded.

"Remember that game his senior year when he returned the interception for a touchdown? Everyone went crazy, cheering their asses off. That was so cool. Ted was so cool."

"Yeah, he was."

Doug folded his arms, leaned against the headrest. "I used to wish he was my brother. I got stuck with an older sister who can be such a pain in the ass. I always wanted a brother."

Randy didn't tell him that being Ted's brother wasn't always as cool as it appeared. Living in Ted's shadow, being ignored for long stretches between those moments when Ted remembered he existed and turned his attention, his effortless charm, to Randy. Little things: playing catch, taking him for ice cream, letting him tag along when he went swimming at the community pool, showing him off to his girlfriends. They were too far apart in age to be really close and Ted died before time could close the gap. But in those moments Ted made Randy feel they shared an unbreakable bond.

"It's so fucked up that he got killed," Doug said.

Randy remembered the May morning he was told to gather his books and report to the principal's office. His father, dressed in the tan cotton suit he wore each spring, his face rigid and pale, stood next to the principal. The clock on the wall read 11:17.

"Your dad is here to take you home, Randy," said the principal.

"Why?"

His father shook his head once and managed a smile that was more of a grimace. "I'll explain when we get home."

Fear settled over Randy like a chill. Through the office window, beyond the green lawn, a white delivery van moved silently down the street in brilliant sunlight. The red sweep hand of the wall clock ticked off the seconds. He walked silently to the car with his father, who rested a hand on his shoulder. Whenever he thought about that day, he felt his father's hand. Solid. Warm. The grip tightened as they walked, as if his father was trying to contain his own fear as well as Randy's.

"Dad," Randy said when they got into the car, "what is it?"

His father shook his head.

They drove home in silence, past the cemetery at St. Paul's where Ted would be laid to rest the following week, down the hill along Main Street past the stodgy buildings. Randy didn't recognize the car parked in front of their house. After parking the car in the driveway, his father sat for a moment staring out the windshield, hands gripping the steering wheel. He drew a breath as if to speak when a sob burst out of him. Randy sat frozen before starting to cry himself. He felt his father's hand on his shoulder and they leaned across the center console in an awkward embrace. After a moment they collected themselves and went into the house. Randy's mother met them at the door and hugged him, her face flushed and streaked with tears, then she collapsed into his father's arms and the three of them made their way to the sofa. Two Marines were standing in the living room. They offered condolences. They explained how Ted had died. IED. It *was* fucked up.

Glancing at Doug, Randy said, "He wasn't afraid of the world."

"He was a brave dude, for sure. Marines aren't pussies."

"I mean he got out of Millwood because he wasn't afraid of the world."

"What are you saying?" Doug shifted in his seat to look at Randy.

Randy shook his head. "Nothing."

They drove in silence a few minutes, the only car on the road.

"I'm not a bad guy," Doug said after a while. "Just because I see things different from you doesn't make me a racist or some shit."

"Did you say you're a dumb shit?"

"Bite me."

• • •

She came into view suddenly, emerging out of the dark—a

woman standing behind a car, leaning over to look at the rear tire on the driver's side. Randy pressed the brake, slowing the truck as they went by. The woman snapped backwards, shielding her eyes with one hand while grasping the trunk of the car with the other.

"Jesus," Randy said. He looked in the rear-view mirror, continuing to slow down.

"You could have hit her."

"We should stop."

"Why?" Doug asked. "She's probably called a tow."

Randy pulled onto the shoulder and started to back the truck up, slowing when it was about ten feet in front of the car, then cutting onto the highway and pulling in behind. He turned on the flashers and looked at Doug. "Then we wait with her until the tow truck comes. It's a woman alone at night on the highway. What if it was your sister?"

Doug smirked.

"Okay, smart-ass, your mom. Whatever. You can stay in the truck if you want." He checked the side mirror before opening his door.

"Shit," Doug said as he yanked his door handle.

The woman was still standing behind the car, an old blue Corolla. The rear tire on the driver's side was flat. The woman crossed her arms as they approached, stepping back from the highway. She was short and slender, with black hair that touched her shoulders. Her dark eyes widened as they reached the rear of the car.

"Do you need help?" Randy asked. Standing on the side of the highway in the middle of the pitch-black countryside illuminated solely by the headlights of Doug's truck, he suddenly felt foolish. They'd probably scared the hell out of her. The woman's eyes shifted from Randy to Doug and back to Randy. She didn't speak.

"It's okay." Randy smiled. "We just want to help." From behind him Doug asked if she had called anyone. When she looked puzzled he held his hand to his ear, pantomiming a phone, and said, "911?"

The woman shook her head. "No." Her voice was small and had a Spanish accent. Randy asked the woman if she needed help, pointing to the tire. From behind him, he heard Doug exhale. The woman nodded. Randy turned back to Doug who shot him a quizzical, furrowed-brow look and whispered, "You know why she hasn't called for help don't you?"

Randy shrugged. "It doesn't matter. We can't leave her."

Doug exhaled a second time. "Shit." He went back to the truck to retrieve a flashlight, walking wide and veering a little onto the highway. Randy called to him to be careful, then gestured to the woman to open the trunk.

It took them twenty minutes to change the tire. The jack in the trunk of the Corolla was rusty but functional. Randy worked it until the flat tire was a few inches above the pavement, then held the flashlight while Doug removed the lug nuts. There was no hubcap, the nuts were also a little rusty, and Doug fumbled a few times getting the socket in place. But once secured he powered them loose with sustained, red-faced tugs, muttering curses. As each one came off, Randy nodded approval at Doug, who mumbled "Fuck you," and "I can't believe you got me into this," but smiled when he pulled the tire off. A couple of cars went by, one in the left lane, the other in the right, sending a backdraft that lifted Randy's shirttail from the back of his jeans and rippled through his hair.

The spare went on quickly. Doug tightened the lug nuts while Randy put the old tire and the jack back in the trunk. Doug stood and handed the lug wrench to Randy, before arching his back in an exaggerated stretch.

"I could use a beer," he said. He grinned at Randy then looked at the woman, who was standing at the rear of the car on the passenger side. She offered a timid smile. "Gracias."

"You're welcome." Doug held her gaze as he stepped backwards. He made a sweeping bow and spun around, the momentum carrying him onto the highway just as he was lit up by the high beams of an oncoming car. The light froze him. Randy bolted forward, shouting to him. Doug stumbled back a step and lurched sideways as Randy reached him and drove him against the side of the truck. The car sped past without slowing, its horn screaming angrily into the night air.

"What the fuck!" Doug gripped Randy by the shoulders, looking at the taillights of the speeding car as they were swallowed by darkness.

"Jesus." Randy leaned against the truck. It was that easy. That sudden. He looked at Doug and shook his head. "Damn."

• • •

Randy drove the rest of the way while Doug polished off the last beer.

"I could have been killed."

"I know."

"Shit." Doug leaned against the window.

They exited the interstate onto the state highway, riding in silence through Chesterton, where only the yellow-orange parking lot lights were on as they passed the mall. Doug had slumped against the window, mouth slightly agape, empty beer can held loosely in his lap. Randy glanced at him, shook his head, and continued towards Millwood. When he reached Doug's house, he woke him. Doug sat up, rubbed his eyes, allowing the beer can to tumble onto the floor.

"I'll drop the truck by tomorrow, okay?"

Doug nodded. He pulled the handle and let the door swing open. Randy asked if he was all right and Doug nodded again, then pivoted and eased himself out of the truck. He turned and stood for a moment, one hand on the top of the door, a slow grin spreading across his face.

"See what you're going to miss?"

He pushed the door shut, slapped the window and walked unsteadily towards the house.

• • •

Two weeks later, he and Doug cut the lawn at St. Paul's and the cemetery for the last time before Randy left for college. Doug drove the riding mower up and down the big expanses of yard and in the rows between the graves, head bouncing to the hard rock coursing through his ear buds, while Randy used a push mower to trim around the graves and the buildings and along the fence. It was late afternoon when they finished and sat on the tailgate of the truck, Doug with a cigarette and Mountain Dew, Randy with a bottle of water.

"I'm going to be screwed without you to do the trim," Doug said. "I fucking hate doing trim."

"Sorry."

"Might have to hire me a Mexican." Doug grinned and took a swig of Mountain Dew.

"Not funny, dude."

"Chill, I'm just kidding." He stubbed his cigarette on the tailgate and flicked it onto the gravel drive.

Randy screwed the cap back onto his water bottle and slid off the tailgate. "I'm going to pay my respects."

The sun threw light and shadow across the cornfield and

sparkled off tombstones as Randy walked down the row of graves until he reached Ted's. He was leaving in two days and felt like he should say something. It was stupid of course, he wasn't going away forever, and it wasn't like Ted could hear him. Still, as he'd been mowing it struck him that today marked an ending. He looked at the headstone, at his brother's name, but no words came to mind. He inhaled the sweet smell of the newly mown grass and looked across the cornfield spread before him like a vast green ocean. He knew what Ted would say: "It's not a big deal."

Yes, it is, Randy thought. *It is.*

Everything Will Be Fine

Billy didn't answer the first call, but the second time his cell phone vibrated on the nightstand, he reached for it, pushed himself into a sitting position and answered. The room was dark except for a slat of gray light where the curtain fell open slightly, like a loosened bathrobe. Deborah leaned across and kissed his chest, resting her hand on his thigh. He caught her by the wrist.

"Where are you? Okay. I'm leaving." He switched the phone off.

"What?" Deborah asked.

He looked at her. "An accident. My older boy's in the hospital." He flung the sheets aside and stood. For a moment he remained frozen, then exhaled loudly and started to pull on his clothes. Deborah slipped out of bed and dressed quietly.

"Sorry," Billy said.

She nodded, touched his arm. "Go. I'll let myself out."

The evening air was chilly, almost cold, as Billy climbed into the cab of his truck. A moment later Deborah emerged, pulled the door shut and walked over to her sister's house. She glanced at him as she crossed the driveway, lifting her hand in a quick wave.

Earlier that afternoon, she had sauntered across the backyard and introduced herself as Peggy's younger sister. Billy had been grilling burgers. When she asked him if he always grilled on Thanksgiving he shrugged and took a long pull from his bottle of beer.

"My ex-wife took my boys to her parents, where I am not

exactly welcome," he said.

Deborah had a round face like her sister, the same blue eyes. She wasn't as pretty, but there was something else, Billy thought, something just as good. He fetched two more beers and she sat opposite him while he ate at the faded red picnic table he had not yet stored for winter.

He told her about his boys, ages five and three, said the worst part of being divorced was not seeing them every day. He hated the idea of custody, the word itself, like his boys were under arrest or something.

He didn't tell her about Stacy or how he'd felt a year earlier when she took the boys and moved into an end unit, three-bedroom townhouse her father helped her purchase, leaving Billy to buy her out of the small ranch house they'd lived in during the seven years of their marriage.

Billy had tried to be a good husband. He had his nights out, but he was a good provider and a good father and kept in shape.

Stacy had let herself go after the boys were born, gaining weight. A little bit after Jimmy, a little more after Stevie. He wanted to say something to her, but wasn't sure what or how. Didn't she know she should take care of herself? Wasn't that part of the deal? As their marriage came undone, Stacy hurled names at him: drunk, cheater. He didn't say what he thought about her weight, didn't call her fat because she wasn't really, just heavier. He didn't tell her that it felt like she had turned her back on him after she had what she wanted from their marriage—the boys—his services no longer needed, thank you. He didn't try to defend himself, but he did imagine her dying or being killed in a car accident.

When the late afternoon light started to fade, Peggy had come out of her house. Deborah waved at her. "I'll be in later. I'm just talking to Billy." Peggy crossed her arms over her chest, clutching her elbows, and looked at them a moment longer before going back inside.

• • •

Stacy was seated in the waiting area outside the emergency room, hands folded and pressed against her forehead, elbows on her knees. She didn't see him enter.

"Hi."

She looked up. In the florescent light her face was pale, washed out, eyes watery and red. Her blonde hair fell even with her jaw-line, unkempt as if she had been running her hands through it. She stood and hugged him, leaning in, allowing him to hold her. She felt thinner and her hair had a faint lemony scent.

"I'm glad you're here."

"What happened?" he asked.

She sat and he took the seat next to her.

"They were going outside to play..."

"Who?"

"Dad and the boys. Mom and I were washing the dishes, the boys were restless, you know how they get. Anyway, Dad was going to take them out in the backyard, let them run around." She gave him a bewildered look as if trying to recall what came next. "Jimmy went ahead of Dad and Stevie. Dad was helping Stevie with his sweatshirt and his shoes had come untied, so Dad was helping him tie them in double knots. Stupid stuff. Jimmy goes out the back door. Dad calls to him to wait, he and Stevie would just be a min-ute. But you know Jimmy." She shook her head, pushed her hand through her hair. "I don't know what happened, Billy. He must have tried to climb on the porch rail."

"Shit," Billy said softly.

Stacy stared at him, not just her mouth but her whole face

trembling, as if on the verge of bursting open. "He wasn't moving."

"Where is he?"

"Intensive care." Her eyes started to tear. "He's in a coma."

Billy shot to his feet, dizzy-headed. He closed his eyes and breathed. This can't be real, he thought. This isn't supposed to happen. He started walking, turned and saw Stacy gathering her jacket and purse.

"Third floor," she said.

Walt was seated in the corner along a row of chairs in the waiting area. He stood when he saw them, hugged Stacy, and offered Billy a weak handshake. He was nearly as tall as Billy, but flabby, with thin, graying hair and thick brown horn-rimmed glasses. He was a retired insurance salesman. He and Billy tolerated each other, but during an argument just before she moved out, Stacy told Billy her father thought he was a bullshit artist. Billy thought Walt was soft.

"Any update?" Stacy asked.

Walt shook his head. "Not a word since they took him back there." He nodded in the direction of a set of double doors on the other side of the nursing station.

Stacy squeezed her father's arm and slumped into a chair along the wall. Billy and Walt sat on either side of her.

"Did you call Mom?"

"Yes. Stevie is asleep."

"Good."

They sat without speaking for several minutes. Billy rubbed his eyes and pressed the heels of his hands against his temples. A nurse came from the other side of the station and they looked up, but she continued down the corridor.

"I don't understand how it happened," Billy said after a moment. He stared at the floor. Light green linoleum with flecks of white.

Walt shifted in his chair and crossed his legs. Stacy watched the nurses' station, as if any news about Jimmy would initiate there.

"It was a freak accident," Walt said. "Little boys do crazy things."

"Yeah, they do." Billy nodded, lips pressed tightly together.

"What?"

"Nothing."

"Say what you're thinking."

Billy looked at Walt. "Little boys do crazy things, especially if they're left alone."

"Billy, please." Stacy said.

"It's okay," Walt told her. "He's right. Maybe if Jimmy's father had been there it wouldn't have happened."

"I don't remember being invited."

Stacy raised her hands. "Please just stop."

Billy rested his head against the wall and closed his eyes. He couldn't let his fat-ass father-in-law get to him. He heard Walt trying to reassure Stacy, his voice a gravelly whisper.

"It's going to be okay. Jimmy will be fine, I know he will."

Billy wanted to call bullshit on him, to ask how he knew Jimmy would be fine. He wasn't a doctor. But when he opened his eyes he saw Walt hunched over in his chair, face buried in his hands. Stacy's hand was on his back mixing small circular motions and gentle pats, like he had seen her do with the boys.

The double doors on the other side of the nurses' station opened and a man in green scrubs emerged holding a metal clipboard. He paused at the station long enough to hand it to a nurse, then continued to where the three of them sat.

"Ms. Henderson?"

It still rankled Billy that Stacy had taken her maiden name back after the divorce. Not the change, but the anger with which she had made it. During one of their last arguments before the divorce was final, she told him he could keep his fucking name; she was giving it back to him.

Stacy stood. "Yes."

Billy rose quickly. "I'm the father," he said. "Billy Pearson."

"Dr. Chada." He extended his hand to Billy.

Walt stood with some difficulty. Stacy put a hand under his elbow.

"Your son had a deep cut to his forehead which required stiches, and a fracture to his right wrist, which we've casted for now. The more serious concern is the blow to the head which resulted in a concussion and some swelling of the brain. We induced the coma to help his brain heal."

Billy felt a rush of anger. He looked at Stacy who continued to face Dr. Chada. Next to her Walt was nodding his head gravely, like he was being consulted or something, as if he had any more of a clue what was happening than Billy did.

"Can we see him?" Stacy asked.

"Of course," Dr. Chada replied, then lifted a long-fingered hand. "But I want you to be prepared. Your son is on a respirator to help him breathe. It is standard procedure, but it can look alarming, worse than it is."

They followed him to the room, Stacy and her father walking side by side, Billy trailing. Dr. Chada pushed open the door and held it for them. Billy met his eyes as he entered and nodded thanks.

Stacy stood over the bed, holding Jimmy's small hand in both of hers. Walt was next to her. Billy stopped at the foot of the bed. Jimmy's body was sunk into white sheets and pillows and surrounded by pale plastic tubing, as if caught in a medical spider web.

Billy stared at his son for a moment, then muttered "Excuse me," and left.

• • •

Stacy found him sitting on a bench outside the emergency room entrance.

"Sorry for running out. I needed some air."

Stacy nodded, took a seat next to him.

"Did the doctor say anything more?" Billy asked.

"Not really. Jimmy just needs to rest, give his brain time to heal."

"How long?"

"Dr. Chada said a day, maybe two. They have to see how he does."

"Your dad still up there?"

She shook her head. "No, he went home to be with Mom and Stevie. He was pretty exhausted."

"Are you going home?"

"No."

"Maybe you should. Get some sleep. There's nothing you can do..."

"I'm not going home, Billy, okay?" Her exasperated tone had a tremulous edge. Billy could tell she was trying not to cry. When they used to argue, no matter how angry he was, hearing that quaver got to him, backed him down.

"Okay. I was just saying."

"I just came down to make sure you were all right."

He looked at her to see if she had really been worried about him or was just being nice. Her expression was blank and weary.

"I'm fine," he said.

She nodded. "I'm going back up."

"Did the doctor ask you before they induced the coma?"

"Yes, of course."

"Been nice if you'd called me."

"I did call."

"To tell me he was in the hospital. Not to ask me about inducing a coma. Jimmy's my son, too, you know."

"I know he is," she said. "I called twice, Billy. Not that I had to. I have custody and it was an emergency and it isn't like either one of us was going to argue with the doctor. But I did call. Check your phone."

He didn't need to check. He'd ignored the first call, hadn't even looked at his phone vibrating on the nightstand, keeping his eyes on Deborah who was already under the covers. "They'll call back," he'd said as he slipped in next to her.

Billy said nothing and after a moment, Stacy stood and went back inside.

• • •

He returned to the house at 6:00 in the morning to shower and shave. Jimmy's condition hadn't changed. From the front door he got as far as the sofa, where he sat, put his feet on the coffee table and dozed. The doorbell woke him. He checked his watch: 6:40.

"I'm sorry, I know it's early, but I saw your truck." Peggy stood with her arms folded across her chest, in jeans and a sweatshirt. She was shorter than Deborah, with flecks of gray in her hair and crinkles at the corners of her eyes.

"Come in."

She shook her head. "That's okay. I just wanted to know how Jimmy is, and Stacy."

Billy nodded. "Well, okay, I think. Jimmy had a fall, cracked his head pretty good. A concussion. He's in a coma."

"Oh Jesus."

"No, no, it's not as bad as you think. They induced it, you know, to help with the swelling, help his brain heal."

"How long will they keep him in the coma?"

"Another day or two. We're talking to the doctor later this morning."

"How's Stacy doing?"

"Pretty good. She's holding up."

Peggy regarded him for a moment. "And you?"

Billy shrugged. "I'm fine. Tired."

"Have you eaten anything?"

"Not yet. I dozed off."

Peggy bobbed her head in a slow, contemplative nod. "I can make you some breakfast."

He sipped coffee at the kitchen table while Peggy stood at the stove with her back to him, frying bacon and eggs. They were silent, the only sound the sizzle of bacon grease. He watched the movement of her arms as she turned the bacon, the tilt of her hips when she shifted her weight. When she was finished, she switched off the burner and deftly transferred the eggs and bacon to a plate which she set before him.

"Thanks."

"You're welcome." She took her coffee mug from the counter and sat.

Billy didn't realize how hungry he was until he started to eat. He finished quickly, biting off half a strip of bacon at a time, scooping glops of egg by the forkful. When he glanced up, Peggy was staring at him.

"Sorry," he said. "I was pretty hungry."

Peggy offered a slight shrug. "I guess I should be flattered."

"It was really nice of you, I appreciate it."

She nodded, sipped her coffee.

"I probably just would have had some cereal or a granola bar, something easy."

She let out a sudden, short laugh.

"Jesus, Billy, you fucked my sister."

Billy wrapped his hands around his coffee mug, stared at the streaks of yellow on his plate, like the crayon drawings of the sunrays Jimmy used to make. He made dozens of them, for a while it seemed like the only thing he would draw. Billy hunched over the table, raised his eyes to meet Peggy's.

"More like we fucked each other, as in two adults doing what they want."

"My sister, Billy, okay? Deborah is my sister."

She stared at him, her head bobbing in the same slow nod as before. For a moment, Billy thought she was going to start crying and his stomach clenched.

"Look," he said softly, "I'm sorry if it upset you. It just happened."

She rose from her chair, placed her coffee mug in the sink and turned to him. "It always does, right, Billy?" And then she left by the back door.

He showered and shaved, put on fresh clothes and gathered his wallet and keys. He and Stacy were meeting Dr. Chada at 10:00. In the living-room, he saw the rays of sun slicing through the window shades and pictured Jimmy sitting on the floor making his drawings.

"He only draws the rays," Stacy had said to him once. They were curled next to each other in bed. She started to cry. He asked her what it was, but she shook her head and burrowed closer to him. Billy remembered how he had kissed the side of her neck and cupped a hand over her breast. When she didn't draw away, he had felt a rush of excitement and relief, thinking that whatever it was, it wasn't his fault.

• • •

He met Stacy in the hospital cafeteria. Like Billy, she'd gone home long enough to shower and change. There were circles under her eyes as if she had applied eye shadow there instead of her eyelids. Even still, she looked good. She'd lost weight. Billy took a seat on the other side of the pale green Formica table where she sat with a Styrofoam cup of coffee.

"Did you eat?" he asked.

She shook her head.

"Can I get you something?"

"No thanks." She offered him a wan smile. Her expression was softer, Billy thought, than it had been the night before. "You can get something," she said. "There's enough time before we meet Dr. Chada."

"I'm okay." Without thinking he almost added, "Peggy made me some eggs," but caught himself. Mentioning another woman was likely to set things off.

Stacy nodded, sipped her coffee.

"Any good?"

She shrugged. "It's caffeine." She took out her phone and started to scroll through messages and emails. He watched her long, delicate fingers slide the screen up and sideways.

"How's Stevie?"

"Okay. Mom and Dad are watching him."

He nodded. "Your dad all right?"

She looked up from her phone.

"What? I can't ask about my father-in-law?"

"Ex."

"Whatever."

She regarded him a moment longer. "He's fine."

He asked if she wanted more coffee and she shook her head. When he returned from buying himself a cup, she set her phone down.

"Do you think it was my fault?"

"What? No."

"I should have helped Stevie so Dad could go outside with Jimmy," she said. "I shouldn't have let Jimmy go out on that porch alone." She started crying, hand over her mouth, shoulders lifting up and down in rhythm with the sobs that rose silently from her. Her face was deep red and Billy feared she wasn't breathing. He reached across the table to hold her hand but she pulled it away, drew a sudden breath as if she had been underwater too long, then composed herself as quickly as she had broken down.

"Sorry," she said, wiping her eyes with a tissue dug out of her purse. "Now I'll look like shit just in time to meet with Dr. Chada."

"You look fine. Better than fine."

"Right." She blew her nose, then took her coffee cup and tissue to the trash can in the center of the cafeteria.

"Stacy," he said when she returned.

"Yes?" She gathered her purse, slipped the strap over her shoulder.

He smiled awkwardly. He used to know just what to say to make things easy between them. Now he searched for words while she waited, staring at him with an expression that betrayed nothing.

"I think Jimmy will be okay," he finally said. "That's all. Everything will be fine."

She nodded, and Billy felt the emptiness of his words hang between them. Then she turned and walked out of the cafeteria. After a moment, Billy followed.

Objects in Motion

The Rutledges had been our next door neighbors for less than a year when Mr. Rutledge entered my life. Nearly twenty years later, I still remember the Saturday morning he crossed from his backyard into ours, where another boy and I played catch with a football.

"You should step into your throw more," he called to me. "Otherwise you'll kill your arm."

I caught the return pass from my friend and turned to Mr. Rutledge.

"Can I show you?"

I flipped him the football. "Sure."

He gripped the ball in his right hand, tapped it a few times with his left, then nodded toward my friend. "Go deep, son, would you?" Pointing to his left knee he said, "Watch my front leg." He turned sideways and took a couple of steps back, gripping the ball in both hands shoulder high. His left foot and right arm moved forward in one continuous motion as he launched the ball in a tight spiral.

"See?" He smiled. "Let your front leg do the work."

Mr. Rutledge was a tall, red-haired man with an athlete's build interrupted by a small paunch. His otherwise handsome face was betrayed by an excess of freckles and a small cluster of acne scars on each side of his chin. I later learned he had been quarterback of his high school team in Pennsylvania. He spent over an hour throwing to us that Saturday as we alternated at receiver and defensive back, then coaching as we took turns at quarterback.

When we finished, he smiled and thanked us for letting him play. Then he told me I had a good arm, that I could play quarterback if I wanted. Over the course of that summer before eighth grade, Mr. Rutledge explained footwork and how to handle the ball, how to step into a throw and to spin the laces of the ball with my fingers to make it spiral. He taught me to lead a receiver by throwing to the spot where the receiver would be when the ball arrived.

My father was shorter than Mr. Rutledge by nearly half a foot, his body round and going soft except for strong hands and thick forearms developed from years of pursuing his hobby of carpentry. He finished the basement in our house and added a screened-in porch. I was his apprentice for these projects, which on spring and summer days felt more like indentured servitude. But despite being antsy on those days he pressed me into service, I admired the grace and strength he brought to this work. He lifted six- and eight-foot lengths of lumber, 2'x 4's and 4' x 4's, as easily as if they'd been made of balsa wood. He sawed with short, powerful strokes and wielded a hammer as an extension of his hand. My own work slowed as I watched him drive nail after nail, the muscles in his forearm cording, the metallic ping of steel-on-steel rising in pitch as the nails sunk into the wood, yielding to the measured, efficient blows.

The only time my father had ever stepped onto a football field was to play trombone in his high school marching band. He had no interest in sports except to watch me. We played catch when I was younger, first with a baseball and later with a football. His throwing motion was herky-jerky, as if his brain sent the movement signals to his body one at a time.

After about twenty minutes he'd nod. "Had enough for today?"

"If you have," I would reply. I never wanted him to think I was quitting on him.

He'd pause a moment, as if reflecting, as if neither of us knew the answer. "All right then." He'd nod again. "Let's call it a day."

By the time Mr. Rutledge crossed into our yard, my father and I had reached an unspoken agreement to stop playing catch. So, when Mr. Rutledge started showing up Saturdays with a football tucked under his arm, my father encouraged me to work with him.

• • •

We lived in a quiet neighborhood about a mile from the high school in Damascus, Maryland, outside of Washington, D.C. Almost all of the houses were two-story, and the yards were big and well-tended. You didn't have to be rich to live there, but you had to have a good job. My father was an accountant at the Department of Agriculture and my mother taught elementary school part-time. Mr. Rutledge was in some kind of sales—real estate and investments. Mrs. Rutledge, a soft-spoken woman with striking green eyes in an otherwise plain face, did not work outside the home. She had been a legal secretary, but quit when their only child, Jessica, was born.

Jessica Rutledge was my age, tall and skinny. She had her mother's dark green eyes and her father's red hair that hung straight on each side of her round face. She was an awkward, dreamy girl, interested in poetry and drama. She told me she wanted to be an actress, but she was never cast in any school plays, partly because she was so soft-spoken, and partly because she was all arms and legs. It didn't seem to discourage her. She still talked about moving to New York to be an actress when she grew up.

"When I get to New York, I am staying put," she said.

She told me her family had moved four times in twelve years because of her father's job.

"He likes to buy and sell houses to take advantage of the appreciation," she explained in a practiced manner.

I didn't think of Jessica as a girl, just someone I could talk to. On summer evenings, we'd sit on my front porch and talk until one of us was called inside. An occasional car passed by on the narrow street. Sometimes on clear nights, I'd retrieve an old Army blanket. We would spread it on the lawn so we could lie on our backs and look at the stars.

"Steve, do you ever think about all the people who have looked at the same stars as we are right now?" Jessica asked me one evening the summer before we entered eighth grade.

I shook my head. "No."

"I do, like when we studied about the explorers this year, you know? And I thought how important the stars were to them to navigate and like they're the same stars that we're looking at."

"Yeah," I said slowly, "that's kind of cool, I guess. I never thought about it before."

"And the moon," she said. "It's the same moon for all of us, you know? No matter where you are. We're all looking at the same moon."

"Yeah, you're right."

She turned on her side and looked at me. "You think I'm weird, don't you?"

"No," I said, turning my head towards her. "Honest. You're different, but you're not weird."

"You don't think I'm a nerd?"

"No."

"Liar."

"Okay," I said. "You're a nerd."

"Thanks a lot."

I laughed and we were quiet for a while. Then she turned towards me again, elbow propped, the side of her head resting against her hand.

"Are we friends?" she asked. "I don't mean like going out or anything. Just friends."

"Yes."

"I'm glad." She stared at me, her eyes wide. There was something too vulnerable in her expression and I had to look away.

"Me too."

• • •

After the first Saturday, Mr. Rutledge and I practiced at a park tucked along one side of our neighborhood where there was more room to run pass patterns. Other boys joined us and even though Mr. Rutledge let them take turns throwing and catching and offered them coaching tips, he focused on me. We walked to and from the park together on those Saturday mornings. There were no sidewalks. Mr. Rutledge carried the football tucked under his arm as we ambled along the side of the blacktop streets. Sometimes he tossed it in the air and caught it or spun it between his hands or gripped it in his right hand and tapped it with his left, as he had done that first day he crossed into our backyard. It was always in motion, a source of energy.

"You played for the Cougars, right, Steve?" he asked me one morning early that summer. Cougars was the name of the youth football team in Damascus.

I nodded. "Yeah. Wide receiver and sometimes cornerback."

Mr. Rutledge tossed the ball into the air. "But you want to play quarterback?" He caught the ball and looked at me.

"Sure," I said without looking at him. "But you know, they have a quarterback. Billy Lawson."

Mr. Rutledge tapped the ball with his hand, then stopped and pointed it at me. "I saw a few of your games," he said. "You have better skills than Billy Lawson. You could be the quarterback next fall if you wanted."

I looked at him. Everything about his face seemed magnified in that moment—the stubble along his jaw and chin, his lips pressed tightly together, the lines in his forehead, the circles under the brown eyes that met mine. My father's face appeared that way to me sometimes, larger than life, but only in moments of anger. Mr. Rutledge was not angry.

Pressing the ball lightly against my chest, he said, "You can do anything you want in life if you want it bad enough." Then he smiled and resumed walking.

"That's what my dad says, sort of. He says the only thing you can control is your attitude, how you react to things."

"Your dad is 100% correct. Attitude is everything. Accept no limits." We had reached the park. None of the other boys were there yet. Mr. Rutledge tossed me the ball.

"It's what I tell Jess," he said. "But it's different with girls."

We started a game of catch to warm up, lobbing the ball back and forth.

"Why is it different with girls?" I asked.

Mr. Rutledge laughed. "I don't know if I can explain it, Steve, maybe your dad can. I just know it is." He released the ball in a tight, flat spiral that reached me quickly. "I'll tell you one thing," he said. "I'm glad she has you for a friend. She needs friends."

I nodded and threw the ball back, matching the trajectory and speed of his pass. "I guess we all do."

"If you're the quarterback you'll have plenty of friends," he grinned. "And plenty of girls."

"Did you?" I asked without thinking. For a moment I feared I had crossed a line, but Mr. Rutledge laughed and shook his head.

"Put it this way, Steve, I did all right." He looked at the ball for a moment, tapping it lightly. "More than all right."

Looking up, he waved his left hand towards me.

"Go deep."

• • •

That fall, Mr. Rutledge became an assistant coach of the Cougars. He coached offense, focusing on quarterbacks and receivers. After the second game, I displaced Billy as the starting quarterback, just as Mr. Rutledge said I could if I tried hard enough. Jessica said she didn't like football, but came to our games. After I became the quarterback, she volunteered to be a team manager, allowing her to stand on the sidelines. I am not sure why she volunteered, but she took the job seriously. She did as she was instructed and tried hard, but not hard enough for Mr. Rutledge. He rarely spoke to her except to order her to do something. Pacing the sidelines he glowered at any player who didn't move out of his way immediately. He glowered at Jessica as well, and more than once he grabbed her by the shoulders and moved her back several steps.

"If you can't stay out of the way, I can't have you on the field," he told her. She nodded and when he turned away, she rubbed her shoulders. One of her jobs during timeouts was to bring the players water bottles.

"C'mon, Jess," he'd call to her. "Move your fanny. The timeout doesn't last forever." Watching them together, I thought for Mr. Rutledge it really was different with girls.

• • •

Sometimes our families grilled out together. My father and Mr. Rutledge drank beer and talked business or politics. Mr. Rutledge was more conservative than my father, but they didn't argue very often. I think Mr. Rutledge would have, but my father wouldn't take the bait. He had a way of smiling benignly, a small upturn of the sides of his mouth without showing any teeth, accompanied by a slight nodding of the head that seemed to end the discussion without conceding the point. He did the same thing when Mr. Rutledge talked about work and marveled out loud at how anyone could stay in an office all day like my father.

"I admire your discipline, George," Mr. Rutledge said to my father. "I sure as hell couldn't do it."

Sitting on our patio one of those evenings late in the summer before Jessica and I started high school, Mr. Rutledge leaned towards my father and suggested an investment.

"I know you're a conservative guy when it comes to your money, George, and I respect that, I do, but you should look into this. It's a great little real estate investment trust, has good tax advantages, and the potential return is excellent. I'll bring over the prospectus later." He sat back in the lawn chair, dressed in khakis, a green polo shirt and docksiders with no socks. He folded his arms across his chest and smiled.

My father nodded, the sides of his mouth moving slightly upward, lips together. "I appreciate your thinking of me, but I don't think I'm interested right now."

Mr. Rutledge tilted his head to one side and shrugged. "No problem. I'm sorry you feel that way though, I think you're missing out on something."

"My loss, then, huh?" My father took a sip of his drink. "Terrific night, isn't it? Nice little breeze." He cast a glance toward the maples, stirring gently in the twilight at the back of our lot.

"No guts, no glory, George," Mr. Rutledge said.

"That's me." My father laughed. Embarrassment for him flashed through me, followed as suddenly by a tinge of guilt. Somehow he was no more concerned about Mr. Rutledge's comment than he was about his Bermuda shorts, black socks, and white sneakers.

"I'm just sorry to see you pass up a good opportunity," Mr. Rutledge continued.

Mrs. Rutledge touched her husband's arm.

Mr. Rutledge shot her a look, and then slowly shook his head, laughing. "Sorry, George, sometimes I get carried away."

• • •

High school started two weeks later and with it everything seemed to change. I made the JV football team as starting quarterback, just as Mr. Rutledge said I would, though he came to only two games. We played on Saturday mornings, and he worked most Saturdays that fall. Sometimes I'd see him on Sundays working in his yard and he'd ask about the team. He'd listen, nodding and smiling, even offering a suggestion from time to time, but looking into his eyes I could tell his mind was on something else.

Jessica came to the games. She sat at the top of the bleachers close to the fifty-yard line, dressed in blue jeans and a sweatshirt that came down to her knees and when it grew colder, a faded brown leather jacket. Occasionally she sat with the other students or with my parents. Yet whenever I looked up from the field and spotted her, she seemed to be sitting by herself, chin resting in her hands, elbows propped on her knees, staring straight ahead.

"Are we still friends?" she asked me one morning as we walked to the school bus stop.

"No, I think you're a disgusting human being and I can't stand to be around you."

"I'm serious."

"So am I."

She stopped walking. "Please stop it, Steve. I'm really asking."

I looked at her. In the early light her face was pale which made her green eyes more luminous. She had done something with her hair so that it was no longer straight, but hung in long, loose curls grazing her shoulders. I would even have said she was pretty except for the way she looked at me, like someone waiting to be hurt.

"Jess," I said, "why do you have to ask?"

"Because I do." Before I could answer she turned away. "Forget it," she said and resumed walking toward the bus stop. I followed, watching her long strides, hands thrust into the pockets of her leather jacket. She nodded to the other kids waiting for the bus but kept to herself. When I reached her I stopped long enough to say, "Yes," before joining a group of guys.

Except for homeroom we were in the same classes and had the same lunch period, but we moved in different circles of our high school society. Just as Mr. Rutledge predicted, as quarterback I could move with any group, sit at any lunch table. I was a jock, but I tried to avoid a jock mentality. Jessica stayed mostly with a group of girls who were smart and got good grades but possessed some flaw—too fat, too skinny, too different— that kept them in the outer circle. I talked to her between classes and occasionally we sat together at lunch. I went out with other girls, I even had a steady girlfriend for a while, but I remained Jessica's friend.

"We're just like planets," she said to me one afternoon as we walked to our lockers after our last class. "We just keep moving around and around and passing each other."

I looked at her. "Who? You and me?"

She shook her head. "All of us. High school."

I nodded slowly. "Okay."

"I think it's sad," she said. "Don't you?"

"I don't know, Jess," I replied as I reached my locker. "I have to go to practice."

. . .

When the Rutledges came to my parents' Christmas party, Jessica and I spent most of the time in the recreation room in our basement watching T.V. We had come upstairs to refill the popcorn bowl and get fresh cokes when we overheard my father ask Mr. Rutledge how business was. They were standing in the dining room near the entrance to the kitchen. I stood closer to the entrance and could see them. Jessica, farther into the kitchen, remained out of their line of sight.

"Not great, George, to be perfectly honest," Mr. Rutledge replied. He took a long drink of bourbon. "'These are the times that try men's souls' as the saying goes." Seeing Mrs. Rutledge approach, he added, "And here is the woman who tries my soul."

"What are you mumbling about?" Mrs. Rutledge asked.

"Nothing, dear, we were just talking a little business."

"Forget business, it's almost Christmas. Time to enjoy."

"Easier said than done," said Mr. Rutledge.

"C'mon, Frank," she said. "Everything will be fine."

"Don't try to cheer me, Doris."

"You need cheering."

"Not from you."

"Frank, please."

"Please what?"

Mrs. Rutledge stared at the floor. After a moment she looked at my father. "I'm sorry, George." She started to walk away but Mr. Rutledge caught her arm.

"Don't apologize for me, Doris," he said evenly.

She looked at his hand on her arm and then at his face. "I was apologizing for myself," she said. "I wouldn't dream of apologizing for you. Now would you let go of me?"

Jessica and I went back down to the basement without speaking. I set the popcorn bowl on the coffee table in front of the sofa.

"Do you want to watch the movie?" I asked. Jessica had brought her family's copy of *It's a Wonderful Life*.

She nodded from her seat on the sofa, and I put the movie in the VCR. When I took my seat next to her she said, "We watch this every Christmas. It's probably my favorite movie."

"Are you sure you want to watch it?" I asked. "I mean, if you are going to watch it with your folks."

"It's okay, I don't think we're going to have time this year." Her voice trailed and she drew her mouth into a smile with her lips pressed together.

"All right," I said. "Let's watch." I picked up the remote and pushed the play button. The RKO radio tower came onto the screen in black and white followed by the old-fashioned credits in neat cursive handwriting. We had turned off all the lights except for a single lamp. I moved the popcorn bowl to the space between us on the sofa and Jessica slid closer, taking a handful.

"This movie makes me cry," she said. "Just so you know." She offered the same tight smile.

"That's okay." I hesitated to put my arm around her in case she thought I was trying to take advantage. But later when she rested her head against my shoulder I didn't pull away.

• • •

My father says money problems can pinch the life out of a man faster than anything and I guess that's what happened to Mr. Rutledge. I saw him a few times that winter shoveling snow and when I waved, he waved back, but he didn't say anything. Jessica said he was working six and sometimes seven days a week. The economy still wasn't very good, she said, and that made it hard for him. When I asked how she was doing, she just replied, "Okay." I must have looked like I didn't believe her. "Really," she said, raising her eyebrows and leaning her round face forward. Then she muttered, "God," and turned away.

"Hey, Jess," I called to her, "c'mon." But she ignored me.

In the spring, she auditioned for the musical and when she wasn't cast, joined the stage crew.

"No surprise," she said to me as we walked home from the bus stop on a Friday in early April. "I really can't sing or dance, and I'm not exactly ingénue material." She laughed. "Of course, I'm not exactly carpenter material either, but I can learn."

"My dad could teach you anything you need to know," I said. "Seriously, he should have been a carpenter."

"I was just kidding. There isn't that much."

We walked quietly for a moment. Jessica gripped the straps of her backpack and looked straight ahead. Her hair was longer, the spiral curls spilling onto her shoulders, and she was no longer all arms and legs.

"I'm sorry you didn't get cast."

She shrugged.

"I don't know about singing and dancing, but I think you could be ingénue material."

She stopped and turned to me. "Thank you. That's a really sweet thing to say."

Now it was my turn to shrug. "It's true."

She stared at me, her green eyes glistening. "It really is easy for you, isn't it?"

"What do you mean?"

"Everything. Football, school, making friends. Being nice. It all comes so easy for you."

"What the hell are you talking about, Jess?"

"You," she said. "Your life." She leaned forward and kissed me on the cheek. "We're not all so lucky." Then she turned and was gone up the driveway and into her house.

The next night, I was coming upstairs from watching "Saturday Night Live" when I heard someone outside shout. I set my popcorn bowl on the counter and listened and when I heard more shouting I went to the living room. The shouts sounded as though they were coming from the direction of the Rutledge house, and looking out the window I could see lights on, but the angle did not allow me to see much else. Then came the scream and I went to the front door and stepped out onto our porch. A moment later the Rutledge's front door flung open and Jessica stumbled out and down the steps of the porch. When she reached the yard she spun around.

"You fucking bastard!" she screamed, fists balled at her side, shoulders hunched.

Mr. Rutledge stepped onto the porch and walked towards her, closing the distance in long, deliberate strides. Jessica stood her ground. He reached her, planted his left foot, and swung his right arm up from his side, catching her full on the side of her face with his open hand.

"Step into your throw," I thought as I watched her fly backwards and hit the ground. Mr. Rutledge stepped towards her and I took off running across the yard. I thought of a different drill as I sprinted at him. Lead with your shoulder, hit and wrap. I crossed into the Rutledge's yard and dipped my shoulder as I reached him, driving into his side. I gritted my teeth, but the impact still snapped my jaw open and shut and I bit my tongue. The warm taste of

blood filled my mouth as we propelled backwards for a couple of steps before tumbling to the grass. My head hit the ground. I saw stars and thought I was going to black out when I heard "You little fuck!" and felt his hands on my shoulders, yanking me to my feet. He gripped my shirt with his left hand and grimaced, spittle at the corners of his mouth, the smell of sweat and alcohol oozing out of him. I heard Jessica scream as his fist hit the side of my face and I went down, swallowing blood and gasping.

"Enough!"

I looked up and saw my father's thick arms wrapped around Mr. Rutledge's chest, pinning his arms to his sides. As I watched, still trying to catch my breath, my father lifted him backwards and threw him to the ground. Mr. Rutledge landed on his side and scrambled to his hands and knees. He started to stand and as he rose he swung wildly at my father who caught the errant fist in his strong carpenter's hand and crushed it like a beer can, pushing Mr. Rutledge's arm down and sending him back to his knees.

"It's over, Frank," my father said.

Mr. Rutledge folded in on himself, his body convulsed in sobs, with my father standing over him. Only then did I notice my father was in his robe and pajamas and see Mrs. Rutledge stepping slowly across the lawn, hand cupped over her bloody nose.

• • •

Jessica finished the last month of school before she and her mother moved to a suburb of Chicago, where Mrs. Rutledge's parents and sister lived. During that month, Jessica and I became more than friends. I held her hand walking to the bus stop each morning and again walking home in the afternoon. We ate lunch together every day. I took her to the spring dance and we held each other through all the slow songs, moving in a small circle. We fell in love, or maybe just discovered we already were.

We talked on the phone almost every day that summer. She didn't know anyone and said she missed me. I told her I missed her too.

"It's okay if you date other people," she said near the end of the summer. "I mean it would be kind of stupid for you not to."

"You too."

"Oh sure. All the boys at Glenbrook North will be hot for me."

"They would be if you'd give them a chance."

"Are you trying to get rid of me?"

"Depends. Are *you* trying to get rid of *me*?"

The line was quiet for a moment.

"Ingénue material, huh?"

"Absolutely."

The next fall I made the varsity. Sometimes on clear nights the moon rose above the football field at the high school. Seeing it, I thought of Jessica and wondered what she was doing then, if she was looking at the moon. When I told her during one of our telephone calls, she laughed and said I was as hopeless as she was.

"It's your fault. You ruined me."

"Oh yeah? I thought I saved you."

"You saved me? From what?"

"Being a stuck up jock."

"I'm not a stuck up jock."

"Well duh."

We stayed in touch through high school and most of our freshman year of college. Nothing happened, we just moved in different directions, as people do. We saw each other a few times after she moved, but those visits have faded from memory. When I think of Jess I remember the night before she moved to Chicago. We walked to the little park along the side of our neighborhood and spread the Army blanket on the slope at the edge of the field. There were no lights and fewer sounds even than on our quiet street. For a long time we lay staring at the stars in sharp relief.

"Can I tell you something?" Jess broke the silence.

I turned to look at her, propping myself on my elbow.

"I really hate him," she said, her eyes fierce in the darkness. "I really fucking hate him." She started to cry, softly at first, then in shuddering sobs that broke like waves against my chest as I pulled her close. I pressed my lips to the top of her head and shut my eyes and held her until she stopped, the sobs replaced by quiet breaths. When I kissed her I felt her cheeks warm and damp against mine.

I don't know where Jess went after we lost touch, but I like to think she made it to New York and found a place to call her own.

• • •

My father came to all my games. He told me once that more than anything he loved to watch me throw the ball, loved to see the moment when I planted my foot and my arm came forward and the ball went sailing through the autumn air in a tight spiral.

"Objects in motion," my father said. "A thing of beauty."

Along the way, we resumed playing catch. I came downstairs one morning on a break from college and found him sitting at the dining room table with my old football in his lap.

"Yeah?" he asked.

"Yeah."

From that day, whenever I come home for a visit, we go out to the back yard and toss the football. It gives us time to talk, to find a rhythm, as we send the ball back and forth in long, gentle arcs. My father's throwing motion has improved so much that I accuse him of practicing when I am not there. He is really pretty good.

Changing Colors

Right after they were seated in a window booth, Phil told Jerry that Julia, the eldest of his daughters, was changing colors.

"Changing colors?" Jerry asked.

Phil nodded. He was in his late forties, a barrel-chested man with dark, wavy hair tending towards gray, a slightly jowly face and old basset-hound baggy brown eyes. He was a rational man, an engineer. He viewed the world as a series of logical components to be assembled into machines and systems that behaved in accordance with fixed rules.

"I know," he said. "Crazy, huh?"

"Well, you're a little crazy, Phil. It's part of your charm." Jerry smiled, but Phil's expression remained fixed.

The waitress came to take their order. She was new, otherwise she could have asked, "The usual?" It was Friday, the one day they didn't bring their lunch or eat in the company cafeteria, but walked the two blocks to the Corner Grill for cheeseburgers piled high with French fries, washed down with a cold draft beer. Neither needed the extra calories or cholesterol, but they enabled each other, rationalizing they deserved a break from canned tuna or the salad bar. Phil ordered a chocolate shake instead of a beer, prompting Jerry to say it must be serious, and when Phil ignored this second attempt at humor, Jerry shook his head and asked what color Julia was turning.

"Darker."

"Well, it's summer, maybe she's just got a darker tan this year. Didn't you tell me she's going to the shore with her friends on the weekends?"

"It's more than a tan, Jerry. I'm telling you, she's changing color. Something is happening." Phil raised his eyebrows and tilted his head towards Jerry, then unfolded his napkin and placed it in his lap. He arranged his silverware—knife on the right, fork on the left—and rested his hands on the table.

"Has Nancy noticed this?" Jerry asked.

Phil shook his head. "She thinks I need to relax."

"Well, you have been busting your ass with the Lennox project."

"Not work," Phil said, screwing his face up in a disgust. "Amir."

"Oh." Jerry nodded. "Julia still dating him?"

"Yeah."

Amir Chaudhry was in the same class at Holy Redeemer Catholic High School as Julia and was attending the same college in the fall. They had been dating for nearly a year. Amir's father was a doctor who left Pakistan in 1995, and Amir was born in the United States. Regardless, Phil didn't trust him. Over lunch in the cafeteria the previous fall, when Julia first started to go out with Amir, he'd told Jerry, "There's a war coming and he is on the wrong side."

"You know I don't buy your 'war of civilization' theory, but even so, how do you know Amir is on the wrong side?"

Phil had fixed Jerry with a sour, disbelieving look. "Please," he said.

"For Christ's sake, Phil, the kid goes to Catholic school."

"His father just wanted him to get the best education, which is not going to happen in the pathetic, unionized public schools. And the diocese needs money."

"And?"

"And it's a marriage of convenience. Do you really think they're giving up Islam?" Phil jammed his fork into a wad of lettuce, spearing a cherry tomato.

"Don't you think that's a little extreme?"

"It's an extreme world," Phil had replied before shoving the forkful of lettuce and tomato into his mouth.

Now he smiled as the waitress brought his milkshake and Jerry's beer.

"Nancy's right, you probably just need to relax." Jerry sipped his beer. "I mean, c'mon, I figured the one good thing about Trump winning was you'd chill out a little."

"Don't be a smartass."

"Can't help it. You know how us liberals are."

Phil shook his head, stuck the straw into his milkshake and took a long pull, eyes cast downward. When he looked up at Jerry, he said, "I don't want to lose my daughter."

"Well, then, don't. Give Amir a chance."

Phil lifted the straw up and down a couple of times before stirring it around the edge of the glass. "There's more than one way to lose a child."

"That may be, but demonizing her boyfriend is guaranteed to drive her away."

"But he's changing her," Phil said. "I can see it."

Jerry laughed. "You think Amir is making her change colors?"

Phil shrugged.

The waitress brought their food and they ate in silence for a moment, savoring the first succulent bites of cheeseburger and ketchup-dipped fries. Phil pointed to his plate and nodded approvingly before taking another long sip of his milkshake.

"It may kill me eventually," he said, "but it's worth it."

"Death by cheeseburger. There are worse ways to go."

Phil took another bite, then lifted his napkin to wipe a spot of mustard from the corner of his mouth. "So, do you think I'm losing it?"

"No," Jerry said. "I think you're worried about your daughter, that's all."

Phil leaned forward, eyes glinting, pugnacious. "Don't get squishy on me, Jerry."

"Okay," Jerry said. "To be honest, you're scaring me a little."

• • •

Sunday brunch was a tradition in the Sweeney household. After returning from eleven o'clock Mass, Phil and Nancy and the girls changed out of their church clothes and prepared a large meal of eggs, waffles, fruit, bacon, coffee, juice, and hot chocolate. Nancy did most of the cooking, but Phil sliced the strawberries and pineapple, the girls set the table and, as they grew older, took over more of the cooking from their mother. They sat around the dining room table holding hands while Phil said grace, punctuating its completion with a more or less unison "amen." Plates were passed, food served, conversation bounced around and across the table. Seated at the head, Phil took it all in, the presence and energy of his family as nourishing as the food for which they had given thanks. Even after the girls were older and more guarded about what they said, more apt to keep secrets and to be embarrassed by their parents, Phil looked around the table and felt renewed.

On the Sunday after he'd confided in Jerry about the changes he saw in Julia, Phil had just set a bowl of fruit on the table when she came downstairs wearing jeans and a black T-shirt with big red letters spelling RESIST. She shot him a quick smile as she entered the dining room and plucked a strawberry from the bowl.

"What's that?"

"What?" Julia answered.

They were on opposite sides of the table. Phil pointed at her shirt, at the letters emblazoned across her chest. "That."

She shrugged. "It's a T-shirt."

"I can see that. What's it doing on you?"

Julia shook her head.

"Well?"

"C'mon, Dad," Julia said. "You know."

"No, I don't. Tell me."

"I'm part of the resistance."

"Really?"

"Really."

Phil walked around the table and stood in front of his daughter. Nancy emerged from the kitchen with a platter of scrambled eggs.

"What's this about?"

"Our daughter is part of the resistance."

Nancy set the platter down. "Since when?"

Julia screwed her face into a disbelieving frown. "Seriously?" Slender, with auburn hair and green eyes, her complexion darker than usual but still perfectly smooth, Phil couldn't help thinking how beautiful she was, and so much more. Loving and kind to her sisters, an honor-roll student, organizer of an annual food drive at her high school, and one of the first altar girls at their parish, an achievement that made Phil proud once he accepted the idea of girls serving Mass. She embodied all of his values, and then she met Amir.

Phil remembered the first time Amir came to the house. Julia had come down to the living room ten minutes before he arrived and perched on the edge of the sofa, scrolling through her cell phone. When the doorbell rang, she'd sprung up to answer it before Phil was halfway out of his chair. Amir smiled as he extended his hand towards Phil, tall, thin, with jet black hair and eyes the color of dates in a dark-skinned face.

"Hello, Mr. Sweeney. It's a pleasure to meet you."

"Likewise." Phil shook his hand, returned his smile. Nancy came into the living room and greeted Amir, and the four of them stood at the door making small talk. Julia said little, shifting her look between Amir and Phil. As Amir chatted about the Nationals, Julia side-stepped nearer to him and slipped her hand into his. The image had made Phil blink.

Now he looked at Julia. "Where'd you get it? Did Amir give it to you?"

"No. I ordered it online."

"Well," Phil said, "I'd appreciate it if you wouldn't wear it in my house, especially not during Sunday brunch."

Julia took another strawberry from the bowl, inspecting it before biting off half. "I'm not staying for brunch."

"What? Oh honey, where are you going?" Nancy asked.

Julia looked at her, then at Phil. "I'm going to a protest in the city."

"Like hell you are." Phil's voice rose.

"Like hell I'm not. I have a first amendment right of free speech."

Phil laughed.

"Sure," Julia said. "Make a big joke out of it. No one laughs at you for going to the March for Life every year." Phil thought she had rehearsed this, preparing a comeback to his objections.

"That's different, I have a moral obligation—"

"So do I!" She turned and started to leave when Phil grabbed her arm. She looked at him, green eyes growing dark. He released his grip.

"My house, my rules," he said.

"Whatever."

Then she was gone, slamming the front door behind her. He turned to Nancy, who stood wiping her hands on her apron. As his younger daughters made their way into the dining room, he took his seat. He smiled at them before bowing his head. "Let's say grace."

The next day Phil told Jerry that Julia hadn't returned. She had gone to the Fergusons, who lived in the same neighborhood as Phil and Nancy and attended the same church. Their daughter Katherine was Julia's best friend. This had happened before when Julia was 13 and Phil refused to allow her to see a touring production of the musical *Rent* because he thought it promoted drug use and sexual promiscuity. The stand-off lasted two days. Katherine's mother gave Nancy frequent updates assuring her Julia was fine, that she and Katherine were hanging out in Katherine's bedroom listening to music.

Then as now, Phil's first instinct was to go straight to the Fergusons' house and retrieve his daughter, even if it meant removing her by force. He wasn't sold on the Fergusons. He thought they were probably the kind of Catholics who would have attended guitar Mass back in the '70s and thought liberation theology was noble. But Nancy had interceded then and now, insisting it was better to wait for Julia to calm down and return on her own.

"Did Julia go to the protest?" Jerry asked. They were sitting in his office.

Phil nodded.

"But she didn't come home?"

Phil shook his head. "Nope. Went to the Fergusons. Sue called Nancy to let her know Julia was there." He looked up with a bitter, knowing expression. "She said Amir dropped her off."

• • •

This stand-off lasted four days. After dinner on Thursday, Phil told Nancy it was time to bring Julia home. Nancy looked doubtful, but didn't argue. Together they walked the two blocks to the Fergusons in silence. Phil rang the doorbell and stepped back, thrusting his hands in his trouser pockets to affect a casual posture. Nancy stood next to him, clutching her arms as if warding off a chill, even though the temperature was in the high seventies. After a moment, Sue Ferguson opened the door and greeted them with a smile.

"Hello."

"Hi, Sue." Nancy dropped her hands to her side. "Sorry to come by unannounced..."

"We're here to get Julia," Phil said. "We appreciate you and Jack providing her a safe place to act out, but it's time for her to come home."

Sue looked at Nancy before inviting them inside. "The girls are upstairs."

"Hey, Phil, Nancy." Jack Ferguson came into the living room. He was the same height as Phil, but with the trim physique of a runner.

"Hi, Jack. We're here to collect Julia."

"So I heard."

"I'll let her know you're here," Sue said.

"Nothing like a teenager to make your life interesting is there?" Jack shook his head.

Phil nodded. "There's always something."

Nancy smiled and resumed rubbing her arms.

"We appreciate you taking Julia in." Phil said.

Jack shrugged. "No worries. I'm sure you'd do the same for us."

Phil wasn't so sure, but said nothing.

"The truth is," Jack continued. "She's a lovely girl and we enjoy having her. She and Katherine are like sisters."

Phil nodded a second time, irritated that Jack talked like this was an extended sleep-over. He heard footsteps on the stairs and looked up to see Sue coming down, followed by Julia, wearing gray cotton running shorts and her RESIST T-shirt. Katherine trailed Julia. His daughter eyed him fiercely as she descended. She remained behind Sue as they crossed into the living room where Phil, Nancy, and Jack stood.

"Phil, Nancy," Sue spoke tentatively, eyes flashing from one to the other before settling on Nancy. "Julia has something she wants to tell you. She didn't want to come down, but I told her that was not negotiable." She stepped aside, leaving Julia face-to-face with her parents. Julia stared at a space between Phil and Nancy, blinked, spoke softly.

"I don't want to come home."

"What?" Phil asked.

Julia looked at him, green eyes flashing a mix of anger and trepidation. "I said I don't want to come home."

Phil laughed, a sudden, derisive burst escaping him like an unexpected belch. He knew it was a mistake, saw Nancy frown and Julia flinch as if she'd been slapped. Jack and Sue tried to remain passive, but Phil read judgment in their expressions.

"This isn't a joke." Julia's face flushed a deep, reddish brown. Phil could see her mouth tremble as she struggled to maintain control. Now was the time for calm, he thought.

"No," he said softly. "It isn't."

"Then why are you laughing?"

Phil glanced at Nancy, who was staring at Julia. He let out a small sigh. "This isn't the time or place, Julia. We can discuss all your grievances when we get home."

"I told you, I'm not going home."

"Oh yes you are."

"I don't feel safe." Julia's voice was a cracked whisper.

Phil stifled the urge to laugh again, then to shout. He looked at Nancy, then at Jack and Sue. All eyes were on Julia. His daughter stood before him, erect, caramel-skinned, eyes glistening with defiance. Who was she?

"Julia? Honey?" Nancy finally managed to say, but Julia did not take her eyes off her father.

When he spoke, Phil enunciated each word slowly, as if holding it up for inspection before releasing it. "You. Don't. Feel. Safe?"

Julia shook her head. "No."

This time Phil didn't care if his laugher angered Julia or upset Nancy or offended Jack and Sue, because there was only so much he could take. "That is ridiculous. Come on," he stepped toward Julia. "We're going home."

"No!" Julia shouted. "I'm not going. The Fergusons said I can stay as long as I want."

Phil shot a look at Jack, who shook his head and held up his hands.

"That's not exactly what we said."

"What the hell did you say?" Phil asked.

"Well, we said she is always welcome here as long as it is constructive."

"Constructive?"

"Yes. You know, constructive, helping you sort out whatever is going on between you."

Phil's head bobbed up and down as if a spring in his neck had snapped. "What's going on is that Julia is changing," he said. "She's becoming someone I hardly recognize. It's bad enough the world is going to hell, but I am not going to stand by and watch my daughter go there too."

"Bullshit." Julia flung the word at Phil.

"Enough," Phil said. "We're going." He grabbed at her arm, but Julia twisted away. As Phil pressed closer, Nancy called his name, but he ignored her and again reached for Julia. Jack stepped between them, arms spread wide, like a referee separating fighters. Phil grimaced and clutched a handful of Jack's dress shirt, feeling the starched fabric crumple in his fingers.

"Jesus, Phil, stop it!" Nancy's voice pierced the living room. Phil dropped his arms to his sides; Jack smoothed the front of his shirt. Nancy stepped around Phil and put her hands on Julia's shoulders. "Get your stuff, we're going home."

Julia slowly shook her head.

"She doesn't have to, does she, Mom?" Katherine had kept a distance, halfway between the stairs and where the others stood, but now stepped forward. Sue frowned at her.

"But you and Dad said..."

"Not now, Katherine." Sue cocked her head at her daughter, eyebrows raised.

"Julia?" Nancy's voice was little more than a whisper.

Phil wanted to take charge, to assert his authority as head of the family. Instead, he felt displaced as he watched his daughter, color rising in her face, a reddish-brown hue that screamed at him as angrily as she had, and Nancy steely calm, the eye at the center of the storm.

Julia exhaled, a loud trembly release of breath, prelude to tears or an emotional outburst, Phil wasn't sure which. Before he found out, the doorbell rang.

"I'll get it," Katherine said.

Everyone remained still while she crossed into the foyer, as if a pause button had frozen them in place. They heard the door pull open and then a startled sound from Katherine, something between a gasp and a giggle.

"Come in, Amir," she said.

Phil jolted to attention, muttered, "Are you kidding me?" and started to step around the others to confront Amir. As Amir entered the living room, Julia lunged into his embrace, staggering him backwards a step. Amir wrapped his arms around her and kissed the top of her head, before smiling at Phil.

"Hello, Mr. Sweeney. I didn't expect to see you here."

"I'll bet not."

The Fergusons moved aside to allow Nancy to step forward and Amir greeted her, too. She nodded in return. Julia turned to face her parents, slipping her arm around Amir's waist, resting her head against his shoulder. Phil knew she did it to provoke him just as surely as if she had yelled "Fuck you!"

"My parents want me to come home," Julia said.

Amir squeezed her shoulder, tugging her closer to him. "Maybe it's time."

"Really?" She turned to him, more puzzled than hurt.

"You can't stay angry forever," Amir said. "It's not good for you."

Phil looked at Julia clinging to Amir, their brown arms intertwined, their brown faces gazing at each other. He wanted to shout, *Does no one else see it? Doesn't anyone see what this guy is doing?* But he swallowed the words, forcing them down like a wave of nausea.

• • •

"Amir actually told her she should come home?" Jerry asked at lunch on Friday after the waitress brought their cheeseburger platters.

Phil nodded as he dipped a French fry into a pool of ketchup. "But he's not fooling anybody. He's too perfect, like that guy Eddie Haskell from *Leave it to Beaver*, you remember? The phony suck-up? Only worse."

"Jesus, Phil. You have to let go of this, it's not healthy."

Phil stared at his cheeseburger, slowly nodding his head. "Et tu, Jerry?"

"What?"

"Are you one of them? Because the Fergusons certainly are, and I am starting to wonder about Nancy."

Jerry leaned back. "What the hell are you talking about?"

Phil took a bite of cheeseburger and stared out the window as he chewed. His reflection in the glass looked pale.

"Listen, Phil, whatever you think is happening, you're mistaken. You need to let this go."

Phil turned back to Jerry. "She hates me."

"No, she doesn't. You're just going through a tough time is all. It'll pass."

"That's what she said when we got home," Phil continued. "She said she hated being in the same house with me, that she couldn't wait to go to college."

Jerry shook his head. "I know that's hard to hear, but kids say things. You're a good father."

They ate quietly for several minutes. The noises of the diner—clatter of plates and silverware, rise and fall of voices, bursts of laughter—exaggerated the silence of their booth, until Phil broke it.

"I'm just trying to protect my family, Jerry."

Jerry nodded. Phil didn't expect him to understand, or the Fergusons, or even Nancy. They were too blinded by optimism, by a belief in happy endings, to see what was happening. But he knew what he saw. He believed the evidence of his own eyes.

The sun was intense when they left the diner. It glared off the sidewalk, the blacktopped street, and the tinted windows of the buildings they passed. The heat wrapped Phil in a smothering embrace, slowing his stride, rendering his skin sticky with sweat. When he looked at his hands and arms they were bleached in the harsh sunlight. He started to speak to Jerry, but as the words left his mouth he felt the heavy air swallow them, dissipating their effect. It was as if he weren't speaking, as if he weren't there.

Old Man Murphy's Boy

Old man Murphy's boy once sang on the Ed Sullivan show. He was a tenor in a Navy choral group that performed "Danny Boy" on the show in 1959. Someone took a picture of the performance, and old man Murphy kept a framed copy hanging on the wall behind the counter of the small gas station he owned. He'd take it down and press a bent index finger under a curly-haired young man in dress blues standing erect in the first row, eyes forward, mouth formed into a perfect oval. "That's Jack," he'd say, "that's my boy. He sang a solo."

The station was two gas pumps and a squat cinder block building at an intersection on the edge of town. The summer after eighth grade, I went there to buy bottles of soda for twenty-five cents, fishing them out of the icy water of an ancient red cooler the size of a dresser, with the words "Coca Cola" stenciled in white cursive letters along the side.

Old man Murphy sat inside in an overstuffed chair of indeterminate color, although some shade of blue seemed most likely. The chair, nearly worn through to the stuffing in spots, engulfed his small, stooped body like the jaws of a giant fish.

"He could always sing, from the time he was a little boy, no more than five or six. He had the purest voice, a real gift. His mother and me, we knew even then it was special, a voice like that. When he was older, he used to sing along with all the songs on the radio, he learned them all, all the words and the melodies. He'd stand in the living room and sing just like he was Mario Lanza or Frank Sinatra. He hit every note just like they did. He still can, of course. He's a fine singer."

Old man Murphy's voice was a phlegmy rasp, a result of age and the unfiltered Lucky Strike cigarettes he smoked one after another. He said Jack didn't smoke. Once when he was twelve, old man Murphy caught him sneaking a cigarette in the small, wooded area behind the house and gas station.

"I slapped that cigarette right out of his mouth, knocked him clean to the ground to boot." He shook his head at the memory. "That was the only time I ever struck him, but by God I wanted to make the point. A voice like that, I wasn't going to have him ruin it with cigarettes."

Old man Murphy lived alone in the house behind the station, a brick rambler with a patch of yard in the front and another in the back leading to the small, wooded area. His wife died when Jack was a senior in high school and the summer after graduation, Jack enlisted in the Navy.

He said Jack got out of the Navy the year after he appeared on the Ed Sullivan show and was living in New York, trying to make a career as a singer.

"He's not much for writing letters, but he calls pretty regular. I told him he should use his GI bill to go back to school, study music if he wants, but get his college." He peered out the window, as if expecting a car to drive up. "But he's doing all right. He's got an apartment with another musician, a piano player. I imagine they're living the life, two young fellas in New York."

• • •

I met Jack Murphy the following summer. I had hardly been to old man Murphy's, as if, having finished my first year of high school, I was too old to spend time drinking soda and listening to his stories. But one July afternoon I felt like a cold soda and rode my bike to the station where, instead of the old man, I found his son.

He was standing behind the counter in the gas station office thumbing through a pile of receipts. He was shorter than I expected, his black hair as curly as in the picture, but thinner on top. His face was fuller, with the beginning of a double chin and a five o'clock shadow. He wore chinos and an open collared, powder blue short-sleeved shirt that revealed thick, pale forearms covered in dark hair. He looked up when I entered, his brown eyes going wide and betraying a trace of annoyance.

"We're not really open." His voice was as smooth and resonant as a radio announcer's.

"Where's old man Murphy?"

He tilted his head. "My father had a heart attack a week ago. He just got home from the hospital yesterday."

"Jesus," I said. "I'm sorry, I didn't know. Is he going to be okay?"

Jack nodded. "If he's not too stubborn to do what the doctor tells him." He came around the counter and extended his hand. "I'm Jack Murphy."

"Tom Johnson, but everybody calls me TJ."

He returned to his receipts. "We really are closed."

"Yeah, sorry. I just came by to get a soda and say hi to old man… your dad."

He nodded towards the cooler. "Help yourself."

I fished a Coke from the frigid water and placed a quarter on the counter. Jack looked up from the receipts and slid the quarter back to me. "On the house."

I came back a couple of times a week after that to see how old man Murphy was doing. Jack was always in the office, most often perched on a barstool he had placed behind the counter, as if the easy chair was reserved only for the old man. There was a radio in the office that old man Murphy turned on to listen to Cardinals' games, but Jack kept it tuned to a classical music station. Once or twice as I approached I could hear him humming to the music, his wordless voice rich and full in the summer air. He didn't stop when I entered, offering a nod hello and continuing until the song ended. He always had a book on the counter, thick novels by authors like Herman Wouk and James Michener. I was surprised to find him working in the station—pumping gas and checking oil, just like his father. He didn't seem like the type, but I guess he felt he had to keep the business going until old man Murphy recovered.

We started to talk more, beyond his telling me about his father's recovery. I asked him what it was like to live in New York, told him it was where I wanted to live when I grew up. I wanted to be an actor. He told me about the people, the thick jam of humanity moving along the avenues and streets every day, the jostle and press, the constant noise, oppressive until it settled into a steady, ever present hum.

"But I'll tell you, TJ, it's the energy that makes it worthwhile. I always feel alive in New York. Not like here. I never felt anything like that in Sangamon, Illinois."

"I guess you couldn't wait to get out. Your dad said you joined the Navy right out of high school."

He was leaning forward on the barstool, elbows on the counter, both hands propped under his chin. "Yeah, I guess so. Things changed after my mother died."

"Were you close?"

He nodded. "She was kind of a buffer."

He said he was trying to make it as a singer anyway he could—in the theatre, records, nightclubs. He had been called back a couple of times for musical auditions on the strength of his voice, but his lack of acting experience hurt him—he had only been in a couple of plays in high school—and he couldn't dance. He and his friend Rick had cut a demo tape, but nothing had come of it so far.

"It's a bitch, don't let anyone tell you otherwise." He drew a cigarette from a pack on the counter.

I laughed. "Your dad said you didn't smoke."

"They're menthol, hardly like smoking at all. You want one?"

I took one from the pack and lit it. I had snuck cigarettes from my parents, but they didn't smoke menthols. The roof of my mouth felt like I was inhaling cool air from a balloon.

"Aren't you afraid your dad's going to catch you?"

He laughed and gave me a quizzical look. "No, are you?"

"He said he caught you smoking out behind the house once and knocked the cigarette out of your mouth."

Jack nodded, exhaling a long stream of smoke.

"He said it was the only time he ever hit you."

Jack focused on rolling the tip of his cigarette on the edge of a beanbag ashtray. "Is that what he told you?"

"Yeah. He said he wanted to make the point so you wouldn't ruin your voice."

He looked at me and grinned, holding up his cigarette. "Well, I guess the point didn't stick, did it?"

• • •

The old man made it to September before suffering a second heart attack. Jack said he died in his sleep, laid down for a nap and never woke up. I saw him a couple of times that summer seated in his easy chair in the office, gazing out the window. He wasn't smoking. "Have you met Jack?" he asked me both times, gesturing at his son, who sat behind the counter reading one of his thick novels. "That's my boy."

The funeral was held at Holy Redeemer. The priest introduced Jack, who stood at the foot of the altar in a dark gray three-piece suit. A piano had been set up to one side and a man I didn't recognize came up from the first row and took a seat on the bench.

"This was my father's favorite song," Jack said. He looked down for a moment, then lifted his head to face the congregation. "Oh, Danny boy," he sang, his voice effortlessly filling the church, tender and pure and brimming with melancholy, as if the congregation had interrupted a moment of private grief.

I was close enough to see the way his throat quavered as he held certain notes, the way his fingers splayed even as he kept his hands at his sides, the way his face contorted with emotion. I couldn't look away. I had never seen a performer so close, so lost in the moment. I felt a tinge of envy for it was what I wanted to do—to sing like that, to lose myself in performance.

Afterwards he introduced the piano player as his friend, Rick, who had flown out from New York for the funeral.

"Finally got in last night at ten o'clock," he said. "Had to change planes in Chicago and catch one of those little puddle-jumpers. It's not easy getting to this charming little burg."

Rick had a trace of a southern accent and spoke deliberately, as if he were reciting lines from a play. He was a few inches taller than Jack, with thick, Brylcreemed blonde hair combed straight back and pale blue eyes. His complexion was pasty and rough and made him look older than Jack, even though they were the same age.

"I'm glad you made it," Jack said.

"Was there ever a doubt?" Rick placed a hand on Jack's shoulder.

We were in the living room of old man Murphy's house, where people had gathered after the service and burial. There was a platter of cold cuts, cheese and crackers, pretzels, chips, beer, wine, and some bottles of Coke, 7-Up and RC Cola that I suspected had been taken from the cooler in the gas station. It turned out to be more food and drink than was necessary, as only a handful of people came to the house.

I noticed on the bookshelf a copy of the picture of Jack on the Ed Sullivan show. As I looked at it I heard Jack's voice from behind me.

"My moment in the spotlight."

"What was it like?"

"Not as exciting as you'd think. It was hot with all the lights and we were in dress uniforms and bunched together."

"Did you meet Ed Sullivan?"

Jack shook his head. "Not really. He said hi to the group, but that was about it."

"But still, you got to sing a solo part on national television."

Jack cocked his head to one side. "How did you know I sang a solo part?"

"Your dad. He talked about it just about every time I saw him."

Jack started to smile but instead his face tightened. He shook his head, wiping each eye quickly. "Sorry."

Before I could say anything, Rick was next to him, reaching an arm around his shoulders.

"Here," Rick said, handing him a glass of white wine. "You need another drink." He tugged Jack closer. "It's all right." He spoke quietly, the soft lilt of his voice bringing out the southern accent.

Not certain what else to say, I told Jack I was sorry. "I didn't mean to upset you."

"You didn't." He gave my arm a gentle pat. "You're a good kid, TJ. I can see why Dad liked you."

• • •

I didn't expect to see Jack again. He and Rick returned to New York. Old man Murphy's gas station closed and the house looked abandoned. I returned for my second year at St. Thomas Aquinas, the all-boys Catholic high school in Sangamon.

I was less intimidated than I had been the previous fall, no longer a freshman at the bottom of the natural order. I was good enough at sports to be picked in the middle of the pack, smart enough to be in the top academic tract, and social enough to have friends in all the groups, even the cool kids at the top of the social order. But I was self-conscious about my desire to be an actor. Among the boys at Thomas Aquinas, it was okay to stand out at sports or in the classroom, but not for theatre, with its makeup and costumes and immersion in the world of make-believe. When I was cast in both the fall play and the spring musical put on by the nearby all-girls Catholic school with help from Aquinas, I tried to keep it low key. After the performances, some guys would come up to me in the hallway or the cafeteria and say "Good job" or "Great show." Even as I thanked them, I searched their expressions for signs they were jerking my chain. When I saw none, I assumed they were hidden beneath the surface, waiting for me to let my guard down.

Early the following June, just after school let out for the summer, I saw a large blue sedan parked in the small drive next to Old man Murphy's house. A week later I went to auditions for "South Pacific" being staged by the Sangamon Players, our community theatre group, and Jack was there.

When I asked why he came back, all he said was he had grown tired of New York. Later, after he had been cast in the role of Lt. Cable and I was in the chorus, we talked more during rehearsals. He said he woke up one day and realized he was thirty years old and going nowhere.

"New York's an expensive place to fail," he said.

"What about the energy you said you always felt?"

He laughed. "It ran out."

Rick had come with him. They both found jobs and were living in old man Murphy's house, which Jack had inherited mortgage free. He sold the gas station.

I listened and smiled, acting as if I understood how he could give up on the dream I thought we shared.

It was the summer before I got my driver's license, so Jack and Rick gave me rides to rehearsal in the '58 Chevy Bel Air they'd purchased second hand after moving to Sangamon. Rick was the rehearsal pianist and later part of the orchestra for the show. He could play anything, classical, jazz, show tunes, and picked up melodies if you hummed just a couple of bars. I sat in the back seat and listened to them talk about the progress of the show, members of the cast, the director. Other times they talked about mundane things: how their days had gone, what to pick up for dinner the following night, whose turn it was to do laundry. Every so often Jack would glance at me through the rear-view mirror and smile, or Rick would turn in his seat to ask me how I was doing.

"Do you have a girlfriend?" Rick asked me one evening as we drove to rehearsal.

"Not at the moment."

"No kidding? I figured you for a ladies' man."

"It's not easy when you can't drive. To go on dates, I mean."

Rick nodded, narrowed his eyes to a squint. "What about Molly Squires? She's pretty cute."

"Very cute. Beautiful in fact."

Molly Squires was an auburn-haired girl in the chorus whose lithe dancer's body had been the object of my fantasies since the first rehearsal.

"Well?"

I laughed. "She's eighteen and going to college in the fall."

"So? I notice you talking to her quite a bit."

"We're just friends. I'm like her younger brother or something."

"I don't think you should quit so easily. I wouldn't."

"Then why don't you ask her out?"

Leaning his head into the back seat, Rick grinned. "If I wasn't so damn old I just might."

Jack laughed out loud.

• • •

The show ran for six performances over the last weekend of July and the first weekend of August. My parents came to opening night. My father told me I'd done a fine job and said he was proud of me. It was an awkward moment, since expressing emotion did not come easily to him, but I thanked him and shook his hand when he offered it.

Jack and Rick came by to say hello. They referred to me in the third person, using words like "talented" and "fine young man," speaking with an enthusiasm that caused my father to blink and draw his head back slightly, as if hit with a sudden burst of light. My mother thanked them for giving me rides to rehearsals. Everyone was smiling, although my father kept glancing at Rick's paisley ascot.

The local newspaper declared us a hit and everyone thought Jack's performance of "Younger Than Springtime" was the best number in the show.

"That's why I wanted the part of Lt. Cable," Jack told me at the cast party the weekend after the show closed. "To sing that song."

It was late in the evening. The party was held at the home of the director; a large, square, three-story house in one of the older neighborhoods of Sangamon. I had come out onto the wide front porch for some fresh air and found Jack sitting on the top step with a glass of wine, smoking a cigarette. His eyes were wide and glassy.

"You did a great job," I said. "I think your dad would have enjoyed it." The air was still but less humid, like a blanket had been removed leaving only a sheet, and carried the aroma of freshly mowed grass.

"Hmmm." Jack's head bobbed a little unsteadily. "You think so?"

I nodded.

"Hmmm," he said again. "It's very kind of you to say. Very kind."

Inside I heard Rick playing the piano and a group singing show tunes.

"It's the truth," I said.

He took a deep drag off his cigarette and exhaled into the night air. "Maybe. My dad and I had a complicated relationship."

We sat quietly for a moment. Inside the group was singing "Bloody Mary," Rick's slightly off-key baritone rising hoarsely above the others.

"Can I say something?"

"Sure." He flicked his cigarette onto the lawn, where the orange tip glowed briefly.

"From what I could tell by the way he talked about you, I think your dad loved you. I know he was proud of your singing."

Jack turned to me and nodded his head. "Maybe so." His eyes welled with tears and I felt his hand on my knee. "You're a sweet kid, TJ." He started to lean toward me, tipping sideways in slow motion, until his head rested against my shoulder. I didn't know if he was making a pass or passing out. I pushed him away and scrambled into the house.

Cigarette smoke permeated the air, and the low murmur of

conversation, punctuated by laughter, mixed with the sound of singing and Rick's piano. To my right as I stood in the entryway was the den where couples and small groups huddled in conversation. Molly Squires, dressed in blue shorts and a sleeveless white blouse, sat in an overstuffed chair facing in my direction, legs tucked under her, one elbow propped on the arm of the chair, the side of her face resting in her hand. She smiled when she saw me, lifting her head and wiggling her fingers in a small wave. For a moment I thought about joining her, asking her for a ride home, and maybe, if I was lucky, stealing an end of summer, farewell kiss. Instead, I smiled and nodded, then turned left into the spacious L-shaped living room where Rick was playing.

There were seven or eight cast members crowded around the piano, an old upright with a black finish, the top of which held a large ashtray and several mixed drinks on paper doilies. The group made room for me. They had switched from show tunes and were finishing "I've Got You Under My Skin" when I wedged into a space behind the piano facing Rick. He bent over the keys at the end of the song, plinking the last few notes with a shoulder-hunching flourish. When he looked up and saw me his face broke into a broad grin.

"There he is, the next great star of stage and screen, Sangamon's own Tommy Johnson. How are you, kid?"

I shrugged, trying to sound nonchalant. "Can I talk to you for a minute?"

Rick cocked his head, brow furrowed. "Sure." He stood and took his drink from the piano top. "Excuse me, folks. Time for a brief intermission."

As we moved through the living room he asked if I was okay.

"It's Jack," I said. "I think he's upset."

He was still sitting on the porch, slumped against the railing, humming or mumbling, I couldn't tell which. He looked at us and his head bobbed in a kind of involuntary nod. Rick sat and put an arm around him.

"You alright?" he asked.

Jack's head bobbed then fell sideways against Rick's chest.

"Okie-doke," Rick said. "Time to call it a night."

• • •

During the drive home I told Rick what happened. Jack was passed out on the backseat, so I sat up front. I was unsure of what to say, hesitated as I described Jack touching my knee and calling me sweet. I alternated between looking at the darkened houses and looking at Rick. His face was in and out of shadow as we passed under streetlamps, but he remained calm, almost passive, as he listened. He kept his eyes on the road.

"I didn't know what to do," I said. "It scared me a little." I was facing forward, watching the road come towards us, the dark reflections sliding up the hood of the car. "Not scared like I couldn't protect myself. I just..." I shook my head.

"You just?" Rick asked quietly, his voice as serene as the neighborhoods we were driving through.

I looked at him. "I just don't want to feel bad about Jack." But even as I spoke I knew it was too late. I'd already started to feel a distance open between me and Jack.

Rick nodded, eyes still on the road, and we drove the rest of the way in silence. After parking in the small drive next to the house, he lit a cigarette and offered me the pack.

"No thanks."

From the back, Jack's snoring sounded like a sibilant whistle. He was curled onto the seat, one arm tucked under his head, the other dangling towards the floorboard.

"He'll feel like shit tomorrow," Rick said.

I nodded.

"How about you?"

"I didn't have anything to drink."

He smiled. "That's not what I meant."

I shrugged. "I'm okay."

"He didn't mean anything, TJ. He's not like that."

"I know."

Rick looked me in the eye. "Do you?"

I nodded.

He squished his cigarette into the little metal ashtray in the dashboard, then opened his door and got out. He opened the rear door and gently tapped Jack on the cheek. When Jack didn't wake up, Rick started to lift him out of the car.

"Do you need any help?" I asked.

"I got it," he said. "You better go on home."

"Thanks for the ride."

There was something in my voice, a hesitation, a forlorn note, that caused Rick to gently lift his hands free of Jack and come around the car to where I stood. He was quiet a moment before pulling me into a hug.

"It's all right," he said. He braced me by the shoulders, his face so close that even in the dark I could see the pockmarks that formed little patterns around his chin and in the hollow of his cheeks. "You didn't do anything, TJ. You have a good heart, that's what got to Jack." His expression was suffused with tenderness. "Okay?"

I nodded, said good night and started to walk home. Before I turned the corner of the gas station, I looked back and saw Rick and Jack leaning against each other. Rick's arm wrapped around Jack's waist, Jack's arm slung over Rick's shoulder, as they stumble-walked towards the little house they shared.

• • •

I never told anyone about that night, because there was no one to tell. Not my parents, who I feared would overreact and forbid me from ever returning to the Sangamon Players, and certainly not my friends at Thomas Aquinas, even the ones who were in theatre with me. Nor was I sure what I would say.

Among the boys at Thomas Aquinas, the slurs "queer" and "faggot" and "homo" were hurled back and forth like baseballs at a little league practice. No one took them seriously because no one thought the words applied to any of us. It was a joke.

I never called Jack or Rick those names, but I started to think them about Jack. They expressed what I had started to feel about him, which was not anger, but a mixture of disappointment and pity that morphed into a kind of contempt. I noticed he always drank too much and talked too loud at cast parties, and that inevitably Rick had to scoop him up and take him home. I saw him as someone who had given up on his dream. Instead of Broadway, he was working as an office manager and performing in community theatre. He had settled for an ordinary life.

I continued with the Sangamon Players until I finished college, and Jack and Rick were always there, part of the troupe. Nothing was ever said of that night, but the memory lingered, like a hovering guest at a party.

After college I didn't move to New York, but I did get as far away from Sangamon as Chicago. Until my parents retired to Florida, I used to go back from time to time. Old man Murphy's station was torn down, replaced by a 7-Eleven; the house was gone too, paved over for a parking lot, but Jack and Rick were still around. I heard they had an apartment near the business district and on weekends they performed in a piano bar on the top floor of the Grant Hotel.

I went once to hear them play. They performed mostly show tunes and American standards, with a few contemporary songs mixed in, and closed the set with "Danny Boy." Jack didn't mention it being his father's favorite song, but he sang it with the same raw emotion he had at the funeral. Eyes closed, arms held away from his body, palms outward, he seemed as lost in the moment as he had that day, and like on that day, I was a little awestruck and envious. Like a participant in a séance where singing was the medium, he was calling on the old man to listen.

When they finished, I bought them a drink. They were both grayer, especially Rick, and Jack had put on weight. After we caught up, after I told them about my wife, my job teaching English in a suburban high school, and the novel I was shopping with agents, the conversation slowly coasted to a halt, like a car running out of gas.

On the drive back to my parents' home, I passed the 7-Eleven that stood where old man Murphy's place had been. I thought about Jack and Rick stumble-walking to their house that night, and I realized I had known what they were without understanding what it meant. I realized that for Jack and Rick, an ordinary life was the point.

Death by Ferris Wheel

Walter Truesdale was terrified of heights. He wasn't sure where this phobia came from. As a child he had climbed trees and jumped off garage roofs trailing a Superman cape, except it was white, not red, and was tied around his neck rather than attached to the shoulders of his shirt. It was, in fact, an old twin top sheet that his mother had cut in half for him. Walter had been fearless as he leapt from the garage to his crab-grassed backyard. He had been a normal boy, free of irrational fears. Now deep into middle age, Walter would argue that a fear of falling off a ladder and breaking his neck while cleaning the gutters was not entirely irrational.

The fear had come on as suddenly as his wife's reflection sometimes appeared in the kitchen window while he stood over the sink sipping coffee.

"Jesus," he'd say, "you need to make some noise."

"Good morning to you, too," she'd reply.

He remembered the day the fear announced itself. He was eighteen and had taken a girl named Linda to the county fair. He'd forgotten her last name. She was somebody's cousin from Chicago, visiting for the summer, and, according to some of the guys Walter hung out with, she was loose. She seemed too nice for that to be true, but Walter thought girls from Chicago might be different. As they walked through the midway eating cotton candy and stopping to play games Walter knew they had no chance of winning, he plotted her seduction. He could tell she was having a good time. She laughed and leaned against him and slipped her hand into his.

Near the end of the evening, as he was thinking about taking her to the parking spot near the lake where he had taken girls during high school, she told him she wanted to ride the Ferris wheel. She said she loved to ride them at night when everything was lit up. Walter felt a little light-headed as the wheel turned through the warm air. Linda rested her head against his shoulder and said she loved seeing the fairgrounds lit up like some kind of magical city. Walter nodded, his dizziness like the buzz he got from a second beer, and was about to slip his arm around her, when the Ferris wheel came to an abrupt halt just as they reached the top.

"Shit," he muttered.

"Are you all right?"

"Sure. Just wasn't expecting to stop." He smiled at her.

"This is so cool," she said. "You can see the lights of the city over there. Look." She pointed with her right hand while resting her left on his knee. Instead of being turned on, Walter was seized with fear that any movement would plunge them to their deaths. It was crazy because they were locked into the seat by a steel safety bar and the seat was bolted to the frame. Still, he had trouble catching his breath.

"Hey," she said. "It's okay if you want to kiss me." She cupped one side of his face with her hand and started to turn it towards her, but Walter's head remained rigid, as if an invisible hand was performing an isometric push against the other side. He gripped the safety bar.

"Are you okay?" Linda asked.

He forced himself to smile. "Just feeling a little weird." Just as he finished speaking, the wheel jerked back into motion. As they descended he felt his breath return, but it was too late. She held his hand on the walk to the car, but when they pulled out of the lot, she told him she needed to go home. She'd promised to get up early the next day to go shopping with her cousin.

• • •

Walter learned to live with his fear. When he traveled for business, he chose aisle seats on planes, and avoided looking down from hotel windows. When his children were young, his wife, Ellen, took them on any carnival ride involving height. Walter claimed to have an inner ear condition that prevented him from taking them. Ellen protected his secret. It embarrassed him, the way being among the last picked for teams when he was a kid embarrassed him, but Ellen said he made too much of it. He was a good man, she told him, a loving father and a good provider. One Monday morning after her wraithlike appearance in the kitchen sent coffee splashing into the sink, Ellen laughed and told him he was overreacting.

"You must be lost in another world," she said.

Walter smiled and took another sip of coffee, trying to affect a casual posture to mask his discomfort at the accuracy of Ellen's comment. He had been in another world, lost in a reverie about Rhonda Radzinski's smile. He thought about the perfectly symmetrical indentation of her dimples, and the flash in her hazel eyes as she laughed at a joke he had made in a staff meeting the day before. It wasn't even a very good joke, but Rhonda's reaction sent a bolt of warm excitement through him, momentarily stirring him out of his work doldrums. Rhonda was a financial analyst assigned to support Walter's team, so there was always a chance she was sucking up, but not as much as if she reported to him directly. Walter guessed she was in her late thirties, although he wasn't very good at estimating women's ages. He'd noticed she wasn't wearing a ring, which didn't necessarily mean she was unattached. Not that it mattered. She was too young for him, too far out of his league even if he were so inclined, which he was not. Office romances always ended in grief—Walter had seen colleagues succumb over the years and come to regret it.

He had remained faithful even though his marriage, like his life, had entered an enervating middle period. He didn't blame Ellen. She was still an attractive woman—aerobics class three times a week and careful about her diet. She still tried, that was the thing, making an effort not just to take care of herself, but to keep some spark in their marriage. She asked about his day, about the stock market, about football, which Walter knew she hated, and she listened attentively to his replies. At night, her hands sought him under the covers. Sometimes he thought she was trying too hard, compensating for his disinterest, and it made him sorry for her. As her hands probed and she climbed astride him, he'd think of Rhonda, which filled him with an excited dread, like daring himself to look out a twentieth-floor window.

Now Walter finished his coffee and set his mug in the sink. "Just thinking about work," he said as he turned to face Ellen. Her blue terrycloth robe was cinched tight and pulled close around her neck, like the turned-up collar of a winter coat. She poured herself a mug of coffee and held up the pot.

"More?" she asked.

"No thanks. I need to shower and get going." He planted a quick kiss on her forehead and started out of the kitchen.

"Walter?"

"Yes?" He stopped at the kitchen entrance.

"Is everything okay?"

He nodded. "Just busy. We have a proposal due Friday."

"Okay." She smiled in a way he used to think of as shy, but that now seemed more knowing, a disguise of some inner calculation.

He left before she could ask more, probe his thoughts, and somehow discover how many contained images of Rhonda. It wasn't just heights that he feared.

• • •

Walter worked late every night that week and Rhonda was there too, crunching numbers to help him figure out a final configuration and price that would be compliant and competitive. It was like working a slide puzzle, pushing the pieces around until the picture fell into place. Rhonda was good at more than the numbers, she understood the business and wasn't afraid to speak up. Walter found himself watching her—the way her blouse tugged against her breasts when she leaned forward at the conference table, the way her dark slacks clung to her hips, and of course, her dimples whenever she smiled. She smiled often. It seemed to Walter that she smiled at him whenever she looked his way, each time sending that same bolt of excitement zinging through his chest.

He ordered pizza and the team took breaks. They talked around the table, and he learned that she was a single mom. Walter felt bad keeping her at the office so late, but she said it was nice to have a break from her routine. She smiled as she said this and raised her eyebrows, as if she were describing a secret rendezvous.

Each night he walked her to her car in the company parking lot, which had decent lighting and was perfectly safe, but he told himself it was the gentlemanly thing to do, and she didn't object. They talked business. He was afraid to venture into anything more personal, concerned his interest might be misunderstood, or understood too well.

On Thursday he told her she was really good, that the proposal could not have been done without her.

"Thank you," she said.

"I mean it, you're the best finance person I've ever worked with."

They were standing next to her car. A nearby street lamp cast a muted light across her face, making her eyes shine.

"I like working with your team," she said. "I like working with you."

"Well, it's a good team."

"And has a good leader."

"Yeah, well." He shrugged. He wondered what she would do if he took her hand in his, if he kissed her. A balloon of anticipation expanded his chest.

She touched his arm. "It's true. Don't sell yourself short."

Walter nodded. He thought about taking her hand, imagined the soft press of her lips. She wasn't looking away and he wondered if that was a sign. He smiled and just as he did car headlights flashed across his field of vision. He blinked, raised his hand to shield his eyes. When the car passed, Rhonda had taken her key from her purse.

"Good night, Walter," she said, flashing her smile a final time.

He watched her car pull away, the red glow of the taillights retreating to the end of the parking lot and disappearing as she turned onto the boulevard, before he walked to his car. He sat awhile, replaying the scene in his head, imagining if he had taken her hand and pulled her into an embrace, her body against his, yielding to his desire. Could it be that easy?

During the drive home, reality overtook fantasy, like light filling a room. He was too old for her, too balding, too paunchy. He was kidding himself if he thought Rhonda's feelings for him extended beyond casual friendship. A blanket of melancholy settled on him. He thought of Ellen, the way she worked to maintain herself and their marriage, with no help from him. He tried to conceal his discontent to avoid hurting her, but feared it seeped to the surface, like sweat through a shirt, carrying its own acrid odor.

Ellen was in bed reading when he got home. She set her book aside and asked him about his day as he undressed. He hoped his brief replies didn't sound terse. He offered a weary smile as he slipped into bed next to her, and said he was exhausted. She nodded, kissed him, and turned out the light on her nightstand.

"Walter?" she said after a moment.

He was on his back, staring up at the dark. "Hmmm."

"Are you okay?"

He felt his heart pound and a rush of dread mixed with an unexpected tenderness. She was facing away from him, the blanket pulled over her shoulders. He thought of turning to her, spooning her the way he once had every night, whispering he loved her. When had he last done that?

"I'm fine," he said. "I'm just tired."

• • •

The proposal was submitted on Friday, but Walter continued to see Rhonda every day. He invented reasons to stop by her cubicle, or to invite her into his office. After disposing of whatever business matters they had to discuss, he struck up conversations. He asked about her daughter, who was eleven and still a sweetheart according to Rhonda, although she knew that wouldn't last.

"All my girlfriends who have teenage daughters say their girls hate them, blame them for everything."

"That sounds about right. My daughter hated my wife at that age. I think she still harbors a bit of resentment, to tell you the truth."

Rhonda shook her head. "That's sad. I hate to think of Kaylee resenting me." She pulled the sides of her mouth into an exaggerated pout, her hazel eyes growing wide.

"I'm sure it's different for everyone," Walter said. "I'll bet you and Kaylee will be fine." He smiled at her. She was wearing a turquoise silk blouse with an open collar. A heart-shaped silver locket hung from a thin chain around her neck, pointing to the cleavage hidden beneath the top button of her blouse. Walter wondered if the locket held a picture of Kaylee.

Over time he learned she had been divorced for nearly ten years. ("My ex was more into making babies than raising them.") He wondered if she was dating anyone, but never asked, knowing it would cross a line. Then one evening at a dinner following a team meeting, he overheard Rhonda tell a couple of women on the team that after a few relationships gone south since her divorce, she no longer felt the pressure to have a man in her life. ("My mom still asks me sometimes, and I just tell her it's not happening.") Walter wanted to interject that not all men were as bad as her ex and the other clowns she had dated, some were in it for the long haul. But he sipped his wine and turned his attention to another conversation buzzing around the table.

Walter lingered outside the restaurant saying goodnight to the team members, checking that everyone had a ride. Traffic had slowed, only a few cars made their way up the wide street to the intersection, their headlights bobbing slightly. A breeze brushed against his face. Rhonda was one of the last to emerge, followed by one of the women Walter had overheard her talking to earlier. They embraced and said good night, laughing at a comment one of them made that Walter could not hear. He waved at the woman, calling out "Good night," then smiled at Rhonda as she approached him.

"Very nice dinner. Thanks."

He nodded. "Glad you enjoyed it."

"I always enjoy getting out." She smiled, her dimples appearing deeper, softer, her eyes a little glassy. Walter wondered if she was okay to drive.

"Where are you parked?" he asked.

"The garage." She lifted her chin in the direction of a structure in the middle of the next block.

"Me too. I'll walk you there."

They started up the block together. Near the intersection, Rhonda was a little unsteady as she stepped over a gap in the sidewalk. Walter caught her by the elbow, then offered his arm.

"Thanks," she said.

There was a Starbucks on the corner across the street. He stopped in front of the entrance and asked if she wanted anything.

"First the arm, now the coffee. Are you worried about me?" She looked at him, tilting her head to one side.

Walter shrugged. "Maybe a little. Plus, I could use one myself."

Inside, Rhonda took a seat at a table by the window while Walter ordered a black coffee for himself and a non-fat latte for her. They sat quietly for a moment. Walter took a sip of his coffee and glanced out the window, then smiled at Rhonda. She was wearing a thin V-necked sweater and the silver heart-shaped locket. The overhead light revealed traces of auburn in her dark brown hair. He started to talk about the meeting, how much he liked the team.

"You're a really nice man," she said.

Walter felt his heart thump like a fist pounding a door. Rhonda's hazel eyes were fixed on him. He looked at the table, saw her hands wrapped around her coffee cup, fingers long and slender, nails painted a pinkish color he could not identify. When he looked up she frowned.

"I'm sorry, I'm not trying to make you uncomfortable."

He shook his head. "It's okay."

"It's just something I've thought for a while, and I wanted to tell you."

"Thank you."

They walked to the parking garage in silence. Walter felt light-headed and focused on taking even breaths to steady his heart rate. He had not offered Rhonda his arm as before, unsure of how she might interpret it, of how he wanted her to interpret it. He smiled at her as they crossed the street and later as they rode the elevator to the fourth level of the garage, and both times she smiled back.

There were only a few cars on the fourth level. When they reached hers, she thanked him for the latte and for walking her to her car. "A true gentleman," she said. He felt like he had in high school at the end of a date, calculating whether to make a move. He felt his heart thump, his body course with desire, as if another man were straining to burst through his skin.

"Good night," he said, his voice huskier than he expected. Then he did it. He leaned forward and kissed her, bracing for her reaction, a push or a slap. Instead he felt her arms circle his neck, her body press against his, her lips part.

• • •

The affair lasted three months: a series of trysts in hotel rooms on business trips, a motel on the outskirts of the city (Walter was afraid of being spotted in a downtown hotel), and once at Rhonda's townhouse when her daughter was spending the weekend with her father. The logistics made Walter nervous. In the hours before each rendezvous, the acid in his stomach churned like boiling soup, his heart zipped and banged in his chest like a bumper car. His anxiety and excitement built to a crescendo until Rhonda, in the flesh, provided relief. Yet the sight of her, naked and voluptuous, caused another trickle of anxiety to leak into his chest as he considered his own sagging physique. Part of him kept waiting for her to burst into laughter and say it was all a joke which she had been recording on her iPhone.

As far as he could tell, Ellen didn't suspect anything. The hotels on the business trips were expensed, and he paid cash for the local motel. Being in sales, he worked long and often irregular hours. Their conversations continued as usual, driven mostly by her efforts, although he initiated more of them than he had previously, and made a point of being cheerful and engaged. A few nights, lying in the dark of their bedroom, he sought her under the covers.

• • •

One day in early August, Rhonda appeared in the doorway of his office.

"I need to talk to you."

"Okay." Walter nodded and gestured, palm up, at the chair in front of his desk.

"Not here. Do you have time for a drink after work?"

"Oh my, sounds serious." Walter smiled.

"More private," she replied, disappearing before he could ask if everything was all right.

They met at a bar on the north end of town, away from the usual after work watering holes. It had become one of their rendezvous spots. Rhonda had texted him where to meet, and he found her in the corner booth they had claimed the first time they met there.

She greeted him with a dimpled smile that seemed as warm as always, except for something hesitant in her eyes. She waited for him to order a drink and take a sip before she spoke.

"I wanted you to hear this from me." She ran one finger along the side of her wine glass, staring at the dark liquid before looking at him. "I've accepted a job in Chicago. I'll be leaving at the end of the month."

For a moment Walter said nothing. He studied her face, which remained calm, her eyes steadily meeting his. She was wearing her silver locket. He remembered it hanging over his face as she bent forward to kiss him while they made love. It turned out there was no picture inside, she just liked the way it looked.

"Well," he said, "I guess congratulations are in order."

"Thank you."

He sat forward. "Rhonda, I hope this isn't about, you know."

She shook her head. "Oh God, no. No. I've been thinking of making a move for a long time. It's a promotion, a management role. Plus, my sister lives in Naperville. It'll be nice to be around family."

"Okay," Walter said. Her dismissal of his concern surprised him. "I just wanted to be sure."

"Walter, this," she said, her voice softening as she made a small wave of her hand in the space between them, "was always just for fun, right? It was never meant to be serious."

He affected a dismissive shrug. "Of course not." He smiled. "I'm happy for you, Rhonda. Really."

"Thank you." She rested her head against the back of the booth. This time when she smiled he didn't detect any hesitation in her eyes, only relief.

They finished their drinks quietly. He felt as if he should mark the end of the affair with a little speech that was pithy and kind and melancholy. Instead he thought three nights ago he'd felt like a man of steel wrapped in a naked, sweaty embrace with her. Now he sat, back to his pudgy, middle-aged self. What, really, was there to say?

He didn't go directly home. He pulled onto the highway that

looped the city and drove in circles for over an hour, passing familiar clusters of commercial buildings and the backs of residential developments. He knew he had dodged a bullet. If their affair continued, something would have gone wrong. They would have been caught. He might have lost his job and Ellen would have left him, taking with her twenty-five years of marriage and the good will of his children, who would surely take their mother's side. No, Rhonda had done him a favor. It didn't feel that way as he glided by pools of phosphorescent light, past the green exit signs, but he knew that in time it would. In time he would feel less foolish, less hurt. He'd get back to himself, back to his life.

The final weeks of being around her in the office were less awkward than he expected. She breezed around as if nothing had ever happened between them, so excited at the prospect of her new job, so happy to be starting a new phase of her life. Walter wondered if the affair had meant anything to her. At her farewell luncheon, the hug she gave him felt perfunctory.

• • •

He and Ellen got away for a long weekend in September. They drove to a resort north of Chicago, almost to the Wisconsin border. They took their time driving, getting off the interstate and wending their way on two-lane state roads. "You can't see anything from the interstate," he said. He liked to drive. The feeling of movement as the countryside sailed by matched his desire to put distance between himself and the affair with Rhonda. The memory of her still made him ache with desire whenever it pierced his consciousness. At the same time, the realization of what he'd nearly squandered was sobering.

He was attentive to Ellen, slowly closing the distance he had allowed to grow between them, relieved that she showed no sign of knowing or suspecting. They listened to classical music on the drive, talked about their children and a remodel of the kitchen they wanted to get started later in the fall. Ellen smiled at him and tilted her seat back, gazing out the window. She was pensive, but that seemed natural. It was a soothing drive on a lovely autumn day.

They passed a carnival on the way, part of a county fair, and Ellen said they should come back after dinner. "We haven't been to one since the kids were little." Walter wasn't as enthused, but he didn't want to spoil the mood by being querulous. So, after they checked in and ate dinner, they drove back.

The carnival was set up at the far end of the fairgrounds, away from the exhibition buildings, a colorful ring of fluorescent lit rides, booths and tents. Ellen took Walter's hand as they made their way through a steady flow of parents with children and teen-agers moving in packs. The sound of organ music meshed with the laughter and screams of ride-goers and the incessant spiel of the barkers. They passed a huge merry-go-round, a tilt-a-whirl, swings flying in circles at the end of chains, bumper cars, and a kiddie car ride. Then, at the edge of the carnival, was a ride that made Walter's heart race: a double-decker Ferris wheel, two Ferris wheels connected by a giant metal arm. He looked at Ellen, who grinned and arched her eyebrows.

"You don't have to go," she said.

But of course, he did. He was a man trying to redeem himself. He couldn't break the romantic spell of the evening by letting Ellen ride alone. He asked the woman in the small red ticket booth for two.

"Are you sure?" Ellen asked.

"Absolutely."

The ride started slow as the seats were loaded, and Walter thought he would be okay. He smiled at Ellen, even laughed as they were lifted higher into the night air. She squeezed his hand. Then the ride began. The Ferris wheel they were on turned in its own arc and then lifted higher in a separate arc as the giant metal arm began to turn. Soon they were spinning and lifting, spinning and dropping as the wheel gathered speed.

Walter looked at Ellen, who had her eyes closed and head back, catching the air. He gripped the safety bar and closed his eyes, but the motion made him dizzy. He watched the ground as they pulled away and descended, pulled away and descended, now lifting higher as they spun, the motion making him feel like he was being tossed between two giant hands. He felt his heart pound and his breath come in short gasps.

"Are you all right?" Ellen was looking at him.

Walter forced a smile. "Not my favorite activity."

The giant arm slowed as it lifted them to the top and then the ride halted.

"Oh God," Walter muttered. He closed his eyes, felt like he was falling, opened them.

"Walter?"

"Shit." He felt like the giant arm was swaying. Sweat trickled down his side, his heart raced in jagged bursts.

"Walter, are you okay?" She gripped his arm and stared at him, her face inches from his. In that moment, he thought, *Did she know? Had she always known?*

He was seized with terror, with the certainty that the Ferris wheel would collapse at any moment, plunging them to their deaths. They would plunge and there would be no Superman to fly to the rescue. He wished he were Superman, wished he could fly. If he could fly he wouldn't be afraid, but he wasn't Superman. He was Walter Truesdale, whose heart was pounding so savagely that he could see Ellen was saying something, but he couldn't hear her. When she put her hand on his chest, it felt like she was trying to crush his heart. He couldn't breathe. He opened his mouth to speak but didn't have enough breath to form the words. He wanted to say he was sorry. He wanted to tell her if she would just stop crushing his chest, he could explain.

Her Brother's Keeper

Growing up in the 1930's, they were taught loyalty to family and a fear of God by their Catholic mother, lessons Maggie had absorbed. Now, thirty years later, she looked at her brother Bill across the oval dining room table—short and thickset with an aura that made him appear bigger than he was, sleeves of his white shirt rolled past his elbows, thick fingers pressed to his temples—and decided it was time to make coffee. The plates and serving dishes had been cleared and washed after the last guests left, leaving a nearly empty bottle of scotch, four whiskey glasses, and a bowl-shaped ashtray the color of strawberry soda. The glasses had a faded gold line around the rim and a black and red coat of arms imprinted on one side. Stubbed and twisted cigarette butts crowded the ashtray, which Maggie took to the kitchen to empty and wash, replacing it with one from a side cabinet.

Her sister-in-law, June, looked at her when she stood, but Maggie made a motion for her to stay. "I'm just going to make some coffee."

June's head bobbed in a half nod. Her hair was pulled back into an unkempt bun, a few gray strands brushing against the sides of her face.

Maggie filled the percolator with water from the tap, measured enough coffee for eight cups into the basket, and plugged the percolator into the outlet above the counter. She retrieved a fresh dish towel from one of the drawers and started to dry and put away the plates left earlier in the drain board. It wasn't fair to leave Hank by himself with Bill and June for too long, but her husband had always been unflappable. She wanted to put the kitchen in order. Putting things in order lifted the spirits, her mother used to say. Poor June wouldn't be able to manage, not today, perhaps not ever.

Maggie leaned against the counter and stared out the window above the sink. The backyard was a dark void except for the light cast from the dining room window, a narrow rim of land at the edge of a black sea. *We wait in darkness for our children to return*, she thought. Four days ago, they'd said good-bye to her brother's oldest children, Bill Jr. and Diane. Maggie waved as they pulled away in a car driven by Diane's boyfriend. A double date, drive-in movie and Fourth of July fireworks. Then she and Hank and Bill and June and the younger children packed the remnants of their picnic and found a spot to spread their blankets and watch the fireworks over the lake. It was well past midnight when Bill called with the news. An accident. A railroad crossing with no lights, no gate, just a sign that was all but invisible in the pitch black. The police said the collision instantly killed the four passengers of the car. *In an instant.*

She had come every day since the accident to cook and keep things picked up and try to provide comfort. Each afternoon before she left she put on a fresh pot of coffee and sat at the kitchen table with June. They said little, but Maggie squeezed her sister-in-law's hand and June nodded, lost and unalterably sad.

Maggie worried about Bill's other children, suddenly unmoored, adrift in a flood of sorrow. Steve, fourteen and now the oldest, had come in after dark with Danny, her eldest, two years younger than Steve. Danny's nose had been bloodied from a fight. Danny had shrugged it off, protected his older cousin, but

Maggie knew what happened. Steve could be a bully, just like his father. When they were kids, Bill had teased Maggie about the way she wore her hair, the way she dressed, her quiet manner. "Mousy Maggie," he'd called her.

"You are your brother's keeper," her mother used to tell her when she complained. "None of this petty squabbling will matter when you're older." It was not a satisfactory response, certainly not the one Maggie was seeking, but she took it to heart and tried to look for the good in her brother, even when his meanness was easier to see. She wanted to see the good in him, to share with him the closeness she believed all brothers and sisters should have.

• • •

Growing up, Maggie and Bill were lucky because their father had steady work. They weren't rich, but as their mother liked to remind them, they never wanted for anything either, not like the poor souls standing in breadlines their mother saw in the newsreels. She saw them in Sangamon too, lined up outside St. Peter's. Sometimes hobos came to the back door of the house and asked if she had any chores they could do in exchange for a meal. Their mother always found something. She didn't allow them in the house, and some days Maggie and Bill would come home from school to the sight of a shabbily dressed man sitting on the back porch eating a sandwich or a bowl of soup.

"They smell," Bill had complained one time, wrinkling his nose in disgust.

He and Maggie were sitting at the kitchen table. Their mother was standing at the stove stirring vegetable soup. She spun around, clutching the large wooden spoon and leaned over the table, her face inches from Bill's.

"They're children of God," she said. "And if I ever hear you speak that way again, I'll have your father give you the belt."

Bill spoke carefully at home after that, but at school he teased anyone who was different, which meant the kids who had less than he and Maggie and the ones who had more. He always said he was kidding, just having fun, but he got into fights anyway. He wasn't big, but he had a mean streak and could hold his own.

• • •

"I don't know what I'm going to do." Bill was looking at Hank when Maggie returned to the dining room with the coffee tray. "What am I going to do?"

Hank turned towards Maggie as she set the tray in the center of the table. His rust-colored hair was thinning and crow's feet appeared when he smiled, otherwise he was as trim and handsome as the day she met him. His light blue eyes were the kindest she had ever seen.

"Bill, you have a family that needs you." Maggie took her seat next to Hank, squeezing his hand. "You have to take care of them."

Bill stared at her, his head tilted slightly to one side, forehead and dark hair shining in the harsh light cast by the bare bulbs of the faux chandelier. "Thank you, Maggie," he said, eyes dull, mouth pulled into a tight smile. "You always did know just what to say."

June said, "Someone has to know." She looked at the table. Her voice was soft, almost a whisper. She lifted her cigarette to her lips, fingers gracefully curved, and inhaled. She held the smoke a moment before exhaling in a steady stream and nodding, as if in agreement with herself.

"That's what I think, Junebug," Bill said. "Someone has to know. But not me. Goddamn if it's me." He ignored the coffee Maggie placed in front of him and instead drank what remained in his glass of scotch.

Maggie sipped her coffee. Bill lit a cigarette and tapped the end absently against the edge of the clean ashtray. Earlier that day when the guests arrived after the funeral, Bill seemed to be at the center of everything, shaking hands, exchanging hugs, accepting condolences. His dark brown eyes darted around as he spoke, always sizing things up, but now he seemed to recede from everything, slumped into his chair, jaw sunk into his jowls, eyes fixed on the curling smoke of his cigarette.

• • •

Once when Bill was twelve and Maggie was nine he went with her and one of her friends to the Saturday matinee, a double feature plus cartoons. They took the bus downtown and Bill had been very nice, no teasing. He'd found a seat on the bus for Maggie and her friend and stood next to them, laughing and talking. He bought their tickets and popcorn and a box of Jujubes for Maggie, her favorite. They watched the newsreel, saw footage of men lined up at soup kitchens, black-and-white versions of the men who showed up at their back door. Then came the cartoons. Bill craned his neck around from time to time, and just as the main feature was starting, he whispered to Maggie that he was going to join some of his friends sitting in the balcony. He told her he would meet her in the lobby afterwards. Maggie looked at him. He grinned and slipped out of his seat and up the aisle. She watched him until he disappeared through the door to the lobby.

In the lobby after the movie let out, he was nowhere to be seen. She and her friend waited for fifteen minutes before asking an usher for help. He led them up to the balcony and stood while they searched for Bill, but he wasn't there. Back down in the lobby, Maggie realized they had no bus fare because they'd given their money to Bill to hold. She started to cry. The same usher asked them what the matter was and when Maggie told him, he shook his head. He took them to the office and let Maggie use the phone to call her mother. The usher told them they could wait in the office, but it was stuffy and smelled of cigarette smoke and stale popcorn. They waited outside instead, leaning against the gray stone building in the fading October light, sharing Maggie's remaining Jujubes, until her father's car pulled in front of the theater. They got into the backseat and rode home in silence.

When Bill came home that evening, he got the belt.

• • •

At the dining room table, slumped in his chair, Bill asked, "Why did this happen, Maggie? Do you know why?"

"No, Bill, I don't. I'm sorry."

"I'm sorry, too." His dark eyes grew watery as if on the verge of tears, but he laughed instead. "I asked Father Cummins why God let this happen and do you know what he said? He said it was part of God's plan and I must pray for understanding. And I said I didn't want to understand a plan like that."

Maggie wished she knew what to say, but acknowledging God's plan and praying for understanding was what her mother would have said. Her mother's devout Catholic faith was the example Maggie turned to in moments of crisis, but her mother never lost a child, let alone two in the same tragic accident.

"I try to live a good life," Bill muttered, "To be a good man. Am I a good man, Maggie?" He stared at her from across the table.

Maggie held his gaze for a moment before answering, seeing his sunken expression and slumped shoulders. "Yes, Bill, you are. Now maybe you and June should try to get some rest."

"And everything will be better in the morning?"

Maggie looked at her coffee, saw on the black liquid surface a reflection of the chandelier. "No," she said. "But you still need to rest."

Bill sat forward, his eyes cast downward on a spot in the middle of the table, as if they were too heavy to lift any higher.

Maggie sipped her coffee. Across from her June had made a pillow of her arms folded on the table and fallen asleep. Hank was nodding off. Maggie kissed him on the cheek and told him to lay down on the sofa in the living room.

"I'm going to check on the children," she said.

• • •

June was once beyond Bill's reach. She was voted the most popular girl in the Sangamon High School class of 1937, Bill's class. Maggie was a freshman that year. Petite, dark-haired, considering herself a plain Jane, she thought June, with her chestnut hair, high cheekbones and azure eyes, was the most beautiful girl in the school. Bill had a wiry frame and thick black hair combed into a pompadour. Maggie heard girls say he was cute, and he always had a date on Saturday nights, but never with June. She later told Maggie that Bill scared her. He had a look, she said, like he wanted to possess her, and a reputation for being fast. Bill thought she was a snob because her father had money.

Three years after they graduated, June had a nervous breakdown while away at college. She returned to Sangamon and was admitted to a private hospital where Bill was an orderly.

"She's not so stuck up now," Bill told Maggie. "Just another mental case like all the others."

"I hope you're nice to her."

Her brother frowned. "I'm nice to her. I even gave her a nickname. Junebug, as in crazy as a Junebug, get it?"

"That's mean."

"No, it's not. It's funny."

June was in the hospital for three months. Bill asked her out the day after she was discharged, although Maggie later learned he had flirted with her while she was a patient. They went to dinner, the movies, and dances in the ballroom of the Grant Hotel in downtown Sangamon. Between dances, Bill kept his arm around June or held her hand. At first, Maggie thought it was a tender gesture, a shield against the stares and judgments of others. June spoke very little, a fragile beauty content to be held. Meanwhile, Bill had something to say to everyone. He told jokes and let loose full-throated, raucous bursts of laughter.

"I'm crazy about this girl," he'd say, giving June's shoulder a squeeze. "But she's just crazy." He told Maggie he was protecting June, making a joke of her condition before anyone else could. Maggie wanted to believe him, but he said it too often, always with the same raucous laugh, until she realized he didn't want June to forget.

• • •

Upstairs there was no light coming from under the closed doors of the children's bedrooms. Maggie listened in front of the one her nieces shared, then carefully opened it. Her two nieces were curled together in one of the twin beds, leaving the other for Maggie's daughter, Linda, eight years old, youngest of the cousins. Maggie closed the door quietly and walked to Steve's room at the end of the hall. After a pause, she cracked the door open enough to peek inside. The room was dark and still, except for the rhythmic sound of breathing, not snoring, but someone in a deep sleep. As she pulled the door shut a whispered voice called to her.

"Mom?"

From the bed nearest the door, the lanky figure of her son rose.

They stepped into the hall.

"Is everything okay?" he asked her once the door was shut.

Maggie nodded. "Yes, I was just checking on you. Can't you sleep?"

Danny shook his head.

He was already six inches taller than her and hadn't stopped growing. She touched his cheek and smiled. "C'mon." They walked to the landing and sat side by side on the top step.

"Is everything okay between you and Steve?"

"Yes. We were just fooling around and it got out of hand." He spoke quickly without looking at her, still protecting Steve, even when it was just the two of them. She wondered how long his cousin would hold sway over him.

"All right," she said, resting a hand on his back.

After a moment, Danny said, "He's pretty upset. He doesn't say much, but I can tell."

"I'm sure he is. It was a terrible accident. I still can't believe it happened."

"Neither can I. It doesn't seem real."

She squeezed his shoulder.

"I've been thinking about it."

"Is that why you can't sleep?"

He nodded.

"Oh, honey."

"I try to imagine what it was like for them."

"Bill and Diane?"

"I wonder what it was like just before the train hit."

It was a terrifying thought. When her mother lay dying in the hospital, she had asked Maggie to say the rosary with her and now the final words of the Hail Mary came to her in her mother's whispery voice: *Holy Mary, Mother of God, pray for us sinners, now and at the hour of our death.*

"You should try not to think of such things," she told Danny.

"Do you think there's something wrong with me if I do?"

She gripped his hand. "No. Of course not. I just don't think you should upset yourself with those kinds of thoughts."

"Steve said I was sick for thinking about it."

"Is that what the fight was about?"

He nodded. He was a few months from being a teenager, a few years from getting his driver's license. Then he'd be out on his own on Saturday nights, beyond her protection.

"There's nothing wrong with you, Danny. Nothing at all. If anyone has a problem, it's Steve."

"Don't tell Uncle Bill, okay? I don't want to get Steve in trouble."

She leaned in and kissed his forehead. "No, honey, I won't tell."

• • •

At Bill and June's wedding reception, there were murmurs of "damaged goods." It was an expression Maggie thought cruel and tasteless, not least because June's father, who owned the largest department store in Sangamon, accepted Bill with calculated resignation, like a man cutting his losses. He seemed to flinch whenever Bill—nearly half a foot shorter—swung his arm up to clasp his father-in-law by the shoulder.

Bill moved through the reception like a man having the last laugh. He kept June on his arm, patting her hand, kissing her on the cheek. He said hello to old classmates, shook hands with the business associates of June's father. They were country club men, part of what Maggie's mother called "the Four Hundred," even though there weren't that many rich families in Sangamon. Maggie wondered where he got the courage, the nerve.

Later, he asked Maggie to dance. He held her a little stiffly, like a boy dancing for the first time. She smiled and moved closer to him.

"I'm happy for you, Bill."

"Thanks."

"I hope you and June will be very happy together." It was something she wanted to say, no matter how ordinary it sounded. Her mother said marriage and family were the source of true happiness and Maggie believed it. She had only recently met Hank but knew she was in love, knew she could be happy with him. She wanted the same for Bill and June.

"We will be."

They found a rhythm, stepped more easily, turned. She felt his hand relax.

"She looks beautiful today."

Bill nodded. "My little Junebug."

Maggie frowned.

"What?"

"Nothing."

"It's just a pet name, Maggie, like sweetheart or honeybun." His voice was petulant, but his eyes had a soft, pleading look.

"I just don't want June to have her feelings hurt. She's a lovely girl."

"No one's hurting anyone, Maggie."

She smiled at him as the dance ended. He made an elaborate bow and offered his arm to escort her back to her table where Hank sat with June.

Hank stood to hold Maggie's chair. June rose and slipped her arm through Bill's.

"Hey, sweetheart," he said. "How's my honeybun?" Winking at Maggie, he steered June onto the dance floor.

Bill took a job as a floor manager in his father-in-law's department store. With a loan guaranteed by his father-in-law, he and June bought a house on the north side of Sangamon, where homes were older and cheaper. It had six bedrooms, a large dining room and an even larger living room, far more room than they needed, but Bill liked the idea of a big house and said they would fill it up. June was pregnant with Bill Jr. when they moved in.

"Welcome to our hotel," she said the first time Maggie visited.

• • •

Downstairs, Hank was stretched out on the sofa, snoring softly. In the dining room, June was still asleep at the table, and Bill remained slouched in his chair, staring straight ahead.

"Come on," Maggie said to him. "Let's get some air."

Bill sat on the stoop in silence, staring into the pitch-black yard. The tips of their cigarettes glowed orange and she could hear the heavy hiss of his breath when he exhaled.

After a moment he asked, "Do you think God is punishing me?"

"What?"

"You heard me."

"Oh, Bill." She squeezed his hand. *The sins of the father.* And what about her, she wondered, her brother's keeper? In the dark she felt him staring at her.

"I don't think God would take Bill and Diane to punish you."

"Then why? Why did this happen?"

She shook her head. "I don't know. I don't think we will ever know."

She would remember this conversation the rest of her life. The ache in her brother's voice, the quiet, unspoken fear they shared that God's wrath, like his love, was personal.

• • •

Maggie visited Bill and June in their new house at least once a week. June told Maggie the house was so big it made her feel lonely. Once after Bill Jr. was born, Maggie sat with her while she nursed him.

"He'll be happy now, won't he, Maggie?"

"Who?"

"Bill."

Maggie leaned forward and touched her arm. "Oh, June, honey, of course he will. He is."

"I hope so, but I'm never sure."

"Has something happened? Did he say something?"

June shook her head. "No. But I always worry I'm not enough." She shifted the baby to her shoulder and gently rubbed his back. "I'm sorry," she said, "I don't mean to bother you."

Maggie shook her head. "You're not bothering me, June." It felt strange to be comforting her sister-in-law, who had everything Maggie wanted—marriage, a family, beauty to shield her from doubt. She smiled and patted June's hand. "Everything will be fine. If my mother were here she'd say you just have the blues."

She visited more often after Hank shipped out to the Pacific. It felt useful to help June with Bill Jr., and a little more than a year later, Diane. A slight heart murmur had kept Bill out of the service. Maggie didn't resent it. She told herself it would not make Hank safer to have her brother in harm's way. She was glad for Bill's company, glad for the growing closeness she felt between them. She hoped they could be brother and sister the way she had always wanted.

On spring and summer evenings during the war, while June gave the children a bath and put them to bed, Maggie and Bill did the dishes, then went outside for a smoke. Bill spoke of how well the business was doing, how he was winning the old man over little by little, just like he knew he would. As Maggie listened, her thoughts turned to Hank, hoping he would have some of her brother's good fortune, enough to bring him home safe.

One evening when June, more tired than usual, had gone to bed right after tucking in Bill Jr. and Diane, Maggie and Bill sat on the porch with tumblers of scotch. They sipped and watched the yellow blink of lightning bugs in the dark. Maggie, who had received a letter from Hank that day full of corny jokes and expressions of love, was flush with whiskey and affection. After Bill had been sitting quietly for a while, she put her arm around his shoulder and asked him if everything was all right.

"Do you remember when we were kids and we did something wrong and tried to hide it and Mom would say there was no hiding from God? God saw all things?"

She grinned. "I remember you doing things wrong. I was perfect."

"But you remember her saying that?"

"Sure. Mom had a lot of sayings."

"Do you think it's true?" He glanced at her.

"I guess so. Why?"

"I've been seeing another woman."

Maggie drew a sharp breath and pulled away as if she'd been slapped. Staring straight ahead, Bill told her it was a woman he had met by chance. He didn't say how. It just happened. They had been meeting at the Grant Hotel. He said it didn't mean anything. It was just that June was so often sad, and he needed a woman who could make him laugh.

"Are you going to leave?" Maggie asked.

He shook his head. "No. I could never do that."

"Then why did you tell me?"

"I don't know, I just felt like I had to tell someone."

"You could tell a priest."

He snorted, shaking his head.

"Or one of your friends."

He looked at her. "I don't really have many friends, Maggie. Not that I trust to keep a secret."

"So, you put it on me?"

"You're my sister."

Is this what it meant to be her brother's keeper, to keep his secret? She didn't think so, but kept it anyway, rationalizing it was to protect June and the children, not to spare Bill. She was ashamed of him, but he was still her brother.

• • •

As she and Hank drove home early the next morning, Maggie looked out the window and watched the houses and yards glide by. She looked at her husband behind the wheel, then at Danny and Linda in the back seat. She smiled at each of them before resting her head against the window and closing her eyes.

It was Sunday. They went to mass early and in the afternoon she and Hank took a nap. The children were somewhere in the neighborhood but would be home in time for dinner. As they lay in bed, she looked at Hank, whose eyes were closed.

"Thank you for last night," she said softly. "I know Bill and June are not easy to be with."

"They're family." Hank didn't open his eyes, but smiled when Maggie leaned over and kissed him on the cheek.

Maggie wanted to ask him if he thought people deserved to be happy, but he would know what she really meant: did *they* deserve to be happy? Could everything they had be taken away? She knew what his answer would be. It was what two years in the Pacific had taught him—you can't ask such questions or even think them.

As she drifted towards sleep, Maggie remembered the time Bill got the belt for leaving her and her girlfriend alone after the Saturday matinee. Their father had pulled him into the den and shut the door before giving him a dozen angry whacks across his backside. Maggie had been able to hear through the furnace register in her bedroom directly above the den. Bill didn't cry, but he'd made a grunting sound, a kind of low moan. Knowing that it hurt him, Maggie had smiled.

The memory jolted her awake. She heard Hank's breathing and through the open window, the distant shouts of children at play. She said a prayer for Bill and June and their children. Then she said one for her own children, praying that no matter what, they would be safe.

No One Left Behind

Tom Griffin's father was a compact man with short black brilliantine hair and dark eyes that held something back even when he smiled. When I stayed for dinner at Tom's, Mr. Griffin would ask how I was doing and how my parents were, and afterwards, on summer evenings, included me in games of catch with Tom and his older brother Greg.

"You need to step into your throw," he'd tell me, and once, when I winced and stepped back on a hard throw from Greg, he shook his head. "Don't be afraid, Pete. It won't bite you." It was hard to tell if he really liked me.

He and my father were friends, though I wasn't sure why. Mr. Griffin was a workingman, a machinist in a Maytag plant that turned out washers and dryers. He told my father he'd grown up hard in southern Illinois, the youngest of five, and that he'd quit high school to join the Navy soon after Pearl Harbor. Afterward he got his GED and learned a trade. My father graduated from college the year before the war started and was the assistant manager of a department store when he enlisted in the Army. On weekend nights during the spring and summer, Mr. Griffin and my father would sit in lawn chairs on our patio drinking beer and smoking. From my bedroom at the back of the house, I heard the low murmur of their voices punctuated by an occasional laugh, but I couldn't make out what they were saying. Sometimes the laughter was longer and turned into something that sounded like crying.

• • •

Tom was eight, the same age as me, and lived directly across the street. Our neighborhood was one of modest ranches and split levels, with large living room picture windows looking out on neat green lawns. It was a new development and some lots stood empty, while others had houses in various stages of construction.

Our fathers' service was a kind of currency for the boys in the neighborhood. One had been a radioman on a submarine, another the navigator on a B-17 bomber. My father had been an infantry captain in the Army. Mr. Griffin served as a cook on a destroyer. Although I never said it, I always thought my father had been the most authentic kind of soldier, most like those we'd seen in movies and who we imitated when playing Army. Lots overgrown with tall grass and weeds were the jungles through which we crept, gripping our toy rifles, while the great piles of dirt left after foundations had been dug were the rugged hills to be taken in our assaults. We charged up the hills until shot, then stumbled and fell to our deaths. Part war game, part imitation of the cinematic deaths we watched at Saturday matinees and on television, we took turns showing off, competing to be the most realistic. We clutched our wounds and fell forward or sideways, breaking our falls with a hand or an elbow or a knee, sometimes sticking where we landed, other times rolling in the dirt to a final death pose. The dirt felt gritty as it pressed against our bodies and worked its way under our T-shirts. Sometimes a hardened clod or a rock stabbed us unexpectedly.

Greg was two years older than Tom and taller, but not as quick or coordinated. He wore black horn-rimmed glasses through which his dark brown eyes appeared magnified and glossy. He got along with the boys his age, but wasn't good friends with any of them, so he tagged along with Tom and me. He was okay except when he picked a fight. He'd call Tom a peckerhead or toss twigs or little bits of dirt at him. They'd start to shove each other and then they were on the ground, grappling, spitting curses, until Greg sat astride Tom's chest, pinning his arms with his knees. When Tom refused to give in, Greg made a fist with the knuckle of his middle finger extended like the point of an arrow and hit his brother in the sternum. He kept hitting him and when Tom still refused, Greg rotated his knees, grinding Tom's biceps until Tom was on the verge of tears and even Greg knew enough to quit.

One Saturday Tom and I ditched him. Tom told me about a fight they'd had earlier over a model airplane that ended when Greg grabbed it from Tom and broke off one of the wings. Greg said he would fix it but Tom shook his head and left.

"I know he's your brother," I said. "But he's a real jerk."

"I wish he wasn't my brother."

We were sitting atop one of the dirt hills next to the skeleton of a new house, throwing small clods of dirt at the wood frame, watching them explode into dust when thrown hard enough. We could see Greg approaching, a solitary figure in blue jeans and a white T-shirt, hand lifted to shield his eyes from the sun.

"I fixed the plane," he said, mounting the hill to join us.

Before Tom answered, I said, "Did you hear something?"

Heaving a clod that smacked against one of the two-by-fours, Tom shook his head. "Nope."

Greg plopped down next to us. "It was pretty easy to glue it back."

"I'm still not hearing anything," I said. "Are you?"

"Not a thing."

Greg stared at us. "C'mon, stop it."

"Do you want to go to my house?" I asked Tom.

"Sure."

We stood and slide-stepped down the hill as Greg watched. I expected him to follow, but when we reached the street I looked back and saw he was still sitting, firing dirt clods at the house.

Tom stayed for lunch and we spent the afternoon in my basement setting up battle scenes with my plastic World War II soldiers. After arranging them behind chair legs, on top of boxes and amid the furrows of the old quilt my mother had given us to mold into a mountain, we killed them, loudly reproducing the sounds of machine guns and exploding artillery shells. When my mother called Mrs. Griffin to ask if Tom could stay for dinner, she was told it was time for him to come home.

The next morning after church, I changed into my play clothes and went to Tom's house. The sun was directly overhead and sparkled off the narrow street, as if precious stones had been mixed into the macadam. The grass was spongy underfoot as I crossed the lawn to the front porch. Mr. Griffin answered the door, still wearing his Sunday suit trousers, white shirt and blue tie. He opened the screen door and stepped onto the porch, which was nothing more than a large concrete stoop at the front corners of which Mrs. Griffin had set clay pots filled with bright red geraniums.

"I'm sorry, Pete, Tom can't come out right now," he said.

The smell of after shave and cigarette smoke clung to him, and his expression contained something more than the usual somberness. As they studied me, his dark eyes oscillated between hurt and anger.

"Isn't Greg good enough to play with you?" he asked.

My face prickled with heat as if it had been slapped. I had to swallow back tears before I was able to reply.

"We were just kidding."

"Well, I'm sorry, but I don't see what's so funny."

He turned and went back into the house.

I didn't go straight home. I walked back to the same lot where we had been the day before, but instead of climbing the dirt hill, I went into the house and sat on the unfinished staircase. A breeze brushed against my face, wafting the scent of pine wood and sawdust. I didn't want anyone to see that I'd been crying.

Later that day, I told my father what had happened. He did not have the reaction I expected.

"You may have meant it as a joke, but it was kind of a mean thing to do."

We were in the part of the basement he used as a workshop. Overhead fluorescent tubes hummed faintly and illuminated the dresser to which he was applying a coat of lacquer. The smell of varnish mixed with the smoke of his cigarette. My father was a tall, lean man with thinning hair and pale blue eyes.

"But Dad, you don't know what a jerk Greg is. Tom hates him."

My father furrowed his brow. "I doubt that."

"He does," I said. "He said he wished Greg weren't his brother."

"But Greg is his brother."

"But Tom wishes I was his brother."

"Did he say that?"

"Not exactly."

My father put his brush on top of the can of lacquer and turned to me. "Don't get between brothers, Pete. You can be Tom's best friend, but you can't take Greg's place. Do you understand?"

I nodded. I didn't fully understand, but I knew that when my father used a certain tone of voice, it was serious.

"I still don't think Mr. Griffin was very nice."

My father took a drag of his cigarette and exhaled towards the ceiling. "He was just defending his son."

"Would you defend me?"

My father smiled. "What do you think?"

"Yes."

"Of course yes."

He snuffed out his cigarette and picked up his brush.

"Anyway," I added, "he wasn't a real soldier like you were."

My father stared at me, brush suspended over the lacquer can. "Peter, I don't ever want to hear you say that again. You don't know the first thing about what Mr. Griffin or anybody else did in the war."

And then he returned to his work.

• • •

As that summer wore on, Tom and I made peace with Greg, even if mine was grudging. I felt like Tom and I had been punished because Greg couldn't make friends with boys his own age, but at least he'd stopped picking on Tom. I stopped complaining about Greg—to Tom, to my father—because I didn't want to get Tom in trouble.

"I won't get in trouble," Tom said when I mentioned it to him.

We were playing in his backyard with balsa wood gliders we'd bought at the grocery store for ten cents apiece. The U.S. Air Force insignia was stenciled in blue on the fuselage, along with the outline of the cockpit and a pilot's head. The wing also had the Air Force Insignia and was fitted through a slot in the fuselage. You could set the wing forward in its slot and do loops or set it back to go straight.

"You won't?"

"Nope."

"I thought you got in trouble that time."

He shrugged, adjusting the wing of his plane to the back of the slot. "A little. But Greg got it worse."

"Why?"

He stepped forward as if throwing a baseball and released his plane into the air, sailing it towards the edge of the yard.

"Greg always gets it worse."

On the other side of a dilapidated wire and post fence marking the southern boundary of our development lay a fallow field of the Jensen farm. In the distance, a white clapboard farmhouse could be seen, and at the far end of the field was a thicket and small stand of trees. "No Trespassing Private Property" signs were affixed at intervals to the fence like rusting, oversized license plates. Jensen lived alone, having lost his son in the war and his wife to cancer. The farm was off limits, but the field had tempted us all summer. One afternoon in the middle of August, we succumbed.

Five of us–Tom, Greg and I, Scott Lawson, and Bill Weaver– gathered by the fence to scout the field before we crossed. Scott and Bill were Greg's age. Bill had his father's binoculars in a black leather case slung to his side by a strap that crisscrossed bandoleer style with the canvas strap of his canteen.

"No sign of him," he announced, lowering the binoculars. "No sign of anything."

"Can I look?" I asked.

Bill's eyes moved from the binoculars to me and back to the binoculars before he extended them with both hands. "Be careful. My dad will kill me if anything happens to them."

I nodded and moved closer to the fence. Lifting the binoculars to my eyes I adjusted the focus until the house filled my vision. The paint was faded, more gray than white, and chipped. A rocking chair on the front porch sat empty. Scanning away from the house I saw a garage with the same faded, chipped paint, in front of which was parked a red pick-up truck. I scanned the empty, sunbaked field between the house and the stand of trees before handing the binoculars back to Bill.

We climbed one at a time, grabbing the post for balance while sticking our toes through the square gaps of the fence like rungs on a ladder. We loped across the field, hunched as if sneaking past a sentry, glancing in the direction of the farmhouse for signs of life. We stepped over furrows, like a series of speed bumps, until we reached the tiny woods. The trees formed a ring and offered shade, while a couple of sprawling bushes provided camouflage. We sat, and Bill passed his canteen around.

"What now?" Scott said.

Bill shrugged. "I don't know. We should bring supplies next time. We could build a lean-to or something."

"We could make a fire ring," Greg added.

"A fire in August?" Bill shook his head.

"I meant later, in the fall."

"Okay," Bill replied, grinning at Scott.

Greg picked up a stick and started to trace circles and X's in the dirt. The air was still, the only sound the rustling of sparrows in the branches overhead.

Bill and Scott argued about the worst way to die in combat, which was really an argument about the most dangerous branch of the service. Everything we knew was from the movies or television; our fathers never talked to us about the war. Bill said the worst would be drowning at sea, being alone in the middle of the vast, dark ocean, treading water until your arms and legs gave out and you sank to the bottom while your lungs burst. Scott said it was being on a plane that was shot down and your parachute failed and you fell through the sky faster and faster until smashing into the ground. I said that getting shot in the gut and bleeding to death would be the worst because you'd have to lie there in agony, bugs crawling on you, unable to move. Bill scoffed at me and said you'd go into shock and not feel anything at all.

Tom interrupted and said, "Getting bayonetted. That cold steel tearing your guts up."

"What does a cook know about bayonets?" Bill asked.

"Shut up, Bill." Greg looked up from his dirt drawings. We were surprised to hear him speak.

"Make me."

Greg's eyes widened behind the thick lenses of his glasses as he stared at Bill. I was waiting for one of them to make a move, when we heard the sound of an engine starting.

Scott scrambled to the bushes and looked across the field.

"The truck!"

Now we all crammed together behind the bush and saw the red truck slowly pull off the driveway and head unevenly across the field toward us.

"Jensen," I said.

"Let's go!" Bill bolted out of the woods into the open field, followed by Scott, then Tom, then Greg and me. We were running full tilt, no pretending to sneak by imaginary guards, no game of Army. I looked back and saw the red truck angling over the furrows, bouncing heavily, clouds of dust billowing from the tires.

It was a race to the fence. Bill and Scott widened their lead over the three of us and got there first. Tom and I were a little ahead of Greg. When we were thirty yards from the fence I looked back at the truck plodding across the field, bearing down, but it wasn't moving fast enough to reach us in time. Bill and Scott scrambled over the fence and looked back. Tom and I made a final push, bounding across the furrows. We were close enough to see the rust on the back of the "No Trespassing" signs when we heard Greg holler.

Tom stopped so abruptly that he stumbled to his hands and knees, before scrambling around to see what had happened. I pivoted and saw Greg writhing in the dirt, clutching his ankle. The red truck was a hundred yards away.

Tom got to his feet and ran back to Greg. I watched the truck bouncing like a carnival ride across the field. Bill and Scott were shouting to hurry, but they didn't come back to help. Greg was up and had his arm over Tom's shoulder as they started to hobble forward. The truck, still fifty yards away, rumbled steadily toward us. Bill and Scott had stopped shouting, and when I looked to where they'd been, I saw they were gone. I ran to Tom and Greg and slung Greg's other arm over my shoulder. Together, Tom and I couldn't run, but we were able to move quickly, carrying Greg as best we could. I didn't look back, but I could hear the truck approaching and the metallic squeak of its shock absorbers. We were at the fence and had started to lift Greg over when the engine stopped and the door opened and slammed shut.

"What in hell are you boys doing?" a twangy voice called to us.

A tall, round-shouldered man in bib overalls and a green John Deere cap approached us. The hair showing beneath his cap was white and his face was an angry sunburned shade of red. His blue eyes froze us where we stood next to the fence.

"I asked what the hell you're doing on my property?"

I looked at Tom, who was staring at the ground. Greg's ankle was swollen and his face looked like he would start crying if he tried to talk. I looked up at the old farmer and told him the truth.

"We were exploring."

"Exploring?" He lifted his cap exposing a bald head over which he ran a large-knuckled hand. "Not much to explore, do you think?"

I shrugged.

"You two brothers?" he asked, pointing his cap at Tom and then Greg.

"Yes sir," Tom said.

"I saw you come back for him," Jensen said. He looked at me. "You too."

We nodded.

"You boys know I could have you arrested for trespassing. That's what the law says. That's why I put those signs up." He gestured once more with the cap, this time at his rusted fenceline.

"I'll let it go this time if you promise never to do it again. Is that understood?"

It was.

"I don't like to reward mischief," he said. "But I don't want to punish loyalty either." Replacing his cap, he lifted his chin toward Greg. "Will he be okay? Can you boys get him home?"

"Yes," I said.

"Okay, then. Better get to it."

He got back in his truck, turned it around, and began his ambling ride back to the house.

Our parents were not pleased to learn we had climbed the fence onto Jensen's farm, but, like him, they let us off with a warning.

I ate dinner at the Griffins' house that night. Greg sat with his ankle wrapped in an ice bag and resting on an extra chair. We told Mr. Griffin about our escape, exaggerating the danger. We said at first we were afraid Jensen might try to kidnap us, but he turned out to be okay. Mr. Griffin listened, sipping a beer from the glass Mrs. Griffin set out for him each night. "Good," he said when we finished. "You boys did good." He nodded at us and when he looked at me, something in his expression loosened.

• • •

The final days of August drained slowly, the air thick and smothering, like an extra layer of gravity. Tom, Greg and I played inside more, partly due to the heat but also because Greg's ankle hobbled him. We played Monopoly or set up elaborate battle scenes with my toy soldiers.

When school started, the rhythm of our lives changed. Tom and I had different teachers so we didn't see each other during the school day except during lunch and recess. After school we played on the dirt hills, taking turns falling and rolling to our deaths, other times climbing on the frames of the half-built houses like they were jungle gyms. Some afternoons we stayed indoors and watched *The Little Rascals* and *The Three Stooges*. Greg watched TV with us, but otherwise joined us less, as if entering fifth grade had caused him to think differently about playing with his younger brother.

Midway through September, after the wasting heat of summer had seeped away, my father undertook a project to enlarge and enclose the patio. One Saturday, a load of lumber was delivered, a mix including four-by-fours, two-by-fours, and large sheets of plywood. Later would come tar paper, shingles, and rolls of screen. That same Saturday, as my father was bringing his tools and saw-horses up from the basement, Mr. Griffin appeared in the yard wearing dungarees and a white T-shirt. He said hello to my father, accepted a cup of coffee, and lit a cigarette while they discussed the project. My father thanked Mr. Griffin for his help, said he couldn't do it without him, to which Mr. Griffin replied that he couldn't let my father have all the fun. And so, each Saturday and most evenings for the next three weeks, the two of them built the screened-in porch.

Tom and I were too young to be of much help, but we did what we could, fetching tools or boxes of nails, moving scraps of wood out of the way, retrieving glasses of ice water from the kitchen. When there was nothing for us to do, we watched our fathers measure, saw, hammer, lift, frame, and brace. Sweat stuck their T-shirts to their backs. Cigarettes dangled from the sides of their mouths, smoke curling up into squinted eyes, the way we imagined it had when they were in the war, the way we had seen in movies and comic books. Their conversation was an easy back and forth about the work, about business, about politics, about the neighborhood, but never about what we most wanted to hear.

On the Saturday after the porch was finished, there was a party. The Griffins, the Lawsons, the Weavers, and a few other couples joined my parents for a cookout and to admire the work my father and Mr. Griffin had done.

"You hire out?" Mr. Lawson grinned.

"You should consider it," added Mrs. Lawson. "I'm not kidding. This is lovely."

My father shook his head. "Too much pressure if someone's paying you. Too much like real work."

"Well hell, Frank, that's easy to fix," said Mr. Weaver. "Do it for free." Everyone laughed, and my mother asked if anyone needed a fresh drink.

The Griffins were the last to leave. Mrs. Griffin helped my mom with the dishes, and from my bedroom I could hear my dad and Mr. Griffin talking on the porch. The murmur of their voices was familiar and I was soon asleep.

I don't remember hearing the phone ring, just waking to a sliver of light under my bedroom door and the hushed sound of my parents talking. I startled them when I appeared at the end of the hallway facing the living room.

"Is everything all right?"

"Yes, honey," said my mother. She was in her nightgown and

bathrobe. My father was dressed in slacks and a T-shirt. "Your father needs to go out for a little while."

"Where?"

"Never mind that now." She smoothed my hair. "Just go back to bed."

A year earlier, my grandmother had died suddenly, the call coming past midnight. That call had been followed by hallway light and whispered conversation, my mother weeping.

"Did someone die?"

My father shook his head. "No one died, Pete. Do as your mother says." Then he nodded at my mother and went out the front door. From my bed, I listened for the sound of the car starting. It never came.

My father was as taciturn about that night as he was about the war. "Mr. Griffin needed someone to talk to," was all he ever said. I knew Mr. Griffin got upset sometimes, especially if he'd been drinking. Tom had told me this, and I'd sensed it at the edge of Mr. Griffin's temper. The real story is not one you would tell an eight-year old, and I didn't hear it until thirty years later, at my father's funeral.

• • •

I was surprised but grateful to see Tom at the service. The Griffins had moved back to southern Illinois the summer after Tom and I graduated high school, after Mr. Griffin had been laid off. Tom and I fell out of touch after the first year of college, but our mothers continued to exchange Christmas cards and occasional letters. Mrs. Griffin was on the list of people my mother called with news of my father's death. She told Tom she wanted to attend the funeral, so he drove her to Sangamon. Greg lived in California and hadn't been back to Illinois in years.

"It was really nice of you and your mom to come," I told Tom at my parent's house after the burial. We were sitting in the screened-in porch sipping beers.

"He was a good man."

I nodded. "He was, but still, it's a long drive."

Tom smiled. He was a taller version of his father, but with his mother's warm demeanor. "You know, Pete, my mom thinks that back when we were neighbors, your dad saved my dad's life. You couldn't have kept her away."

I stared at him.

"Did you ever hear the story?"

I shook my head and sipped my beer.

"Why am I not surprised? I didn't hear it until after my dad passed away. Mom told me."

Tom said the destroyer his dad served on was sunk by a kamikaze. When the plane struck Mr. Griffin was at his battle station manning an anti-aircraft gun—it turned out everyone on the ship had a battle station, even the cooks. Mr. Griffin was thrown to the deck by the explosion. He was on all fours trying to keep his head from spinning, fire and smoke everywhere, when he heard screams. He got up, unable to see because of the smoke, and followed the sound, only now it was behind him. He turned and went a few steps, and it was behind him again. The screams were everywhere. Mr. Griffin stood there, not knowing which way to go. Then another sailor grabbed him and said the ship was going down and they needed to get into a life raft.

"Jesus," I said.

"Yeah. Over a hundred men went down with the ship. Mom said Dad used to wake up in the middle of the night, just kind of jolt awake. When she asked him what was wrong, he said the screams woke him. She said sometimes he'd cry. Other times he'd lie there, staring at the ceiling. He had some kind of survivor's guilt, but I think his emotions embarrassed him, you know?"

"They never talked about that stuff."

"The only people Dad ever told were my mom and your dad. Mom said that's what saved him, having your dad to talk to. She told me there were plenty of times she worried he might harm himself. That's the way she put it, harm himself, but I knew what she meant. She said he'd get so bottled up. 'Talk to Frank,' she'd tell him. 'Go on over and talk to Frank.'" Tom smiled. "There was something about your dad."

I nodded, the day's sadness seeping through me again.

"Did you have any idea?" I asked.

Tom stared at his bottle of beer. "He could be moody sometimes." He sat very still for a moment and I thought he might leave it there, then he looked at me. "He could be scary, Pete. He'd just explode, get after us about finishing a chore or doing something Mom asked us to do, or just anything that parents get on their kids about. Except he'd just go off. Yelling that we had no idea how lucky we were, how good we had it. He'd go on and on, like he didn't know how to stop. Like he couldn't stop until he got it all out."

He tapped the side of his beer bottle. "At least he never hit us. I was always afraid he was going to, more so Greg than me. He was always tougher on Greg."

When I asked him why, Tom shook his head. "I don't know. Maybe because he was the oldest? Plus, you know how Greg was always a bit of a loner. I think that worried Dad. I think he felt like he had to push him to make friends, to get along. Not that it did any good."

Tom told me they rarely spoke. Greg had served four years in the Navy during Vietnam, then attended three colleges before getting a degree. Twice divorced, he was living alone and working in a research lab in Sacramento. Tom had last seen him at their father's funeral.

"Does he ever write or anything?"

"Not really, but I call him every couple of months just to annoy him." Tom smiled.

From inside, I could hear the quiet lilt of our mothers' voices. Through the screen came the insistent chirping of crickets, like white noise. I thought of my father and Mr. Griffin sitting out here when it was still a patio, the muffled traces of their conversation. Glancing around, I remembered the two of them building the porch. Late one Saturday afternoon that September, Mr. Griffin missed a nail and hammered his thumb instead.

"Goddamnit!" he shouted, gripping his thumb, hammer clanging onto the concrete floor. Tom and I froze.

"Are you okay?" my dad asked. "I know that hurts."

"Like a son-of-a-bitch," Mr. Griffin said. Then he looked at Tom and me. "Sorry, boys, sometimes curse words come out before I know it."

"That's okay," I said.

"Oh yeah?" Mr. Griffin's eyes widened as they met mine. "Well as long as you say so." He patted my shoulder and chuckled and the chuckle grew into a laugh, and then we all laughed, men and boys, fathers and sons, and we kept laughing until the two of them went back to work.

The Hat

When he was six years old, Bill wore a red cowboy hat everywhere except at the dinner table and to bed. He wore it on the Saturday a new family moved into the house that backed up to the empty lot next to his. He and his father were raking leaves in the front yard. His father paused, leaned on his rake, and stared across the empty lot at the children scurrying around.

"Huh," his father said.

Leaning on the child's rake his father had fashioned for him by sawing half the handle off an older one, Bill said, "Huh," drawing a smile from his father. A Black woman in a yellow dress stepped out onto the back stoop of the house and called to the children, who scrambled inside. Bill's father resumed raking.

In the early afternoon, his father burned leaves in a large steel barrel in their back yard. Plumes of gray smoke billowed upward and a pungent odor hung in the air. Bill watched for a while, then wandered to the front yard. Across the empty lot, a boy was tossing a baseball into the air and catching it. He stopped when he saw Bill approach.

"Hi," Bill said.

The boy nodded. "Hello." He looked to be Bill's age. He wore blue jeans with patches on the knees and black high-top sneakers.

"My name is Bill."

"Ronny."

"Are you going to live here now?"

Ronny nodded, eyeing Bill's hat.

"I live over there." Bill pointed back towards his house.

"Uh-huh. I seen you earlier." Ronny tossed the baseball above his head, then stepped back and caught it.

"Do you play baseball?"

Ronny shook his head. "Do you?"

"Not yet. My dad says I can try out for Little League next summer if I want to."

"Do you?"

Bill shrugged. Ronny tossed his baseball into the air again and caught it.

"Can I try?" Bill asked.

Ronny looked at him. "Can I see your hat?"

Bill thought for a moment. He had never let anyone touch his hat, not even his best friend Pete, who lived two doors down in the other direction. Of course, Pete had his own cowboy hat.

"I won't do anything to it," Ronny said. "I just want to try it on."

Bill nodded and they made the exchange. Bill flipped the ball between his hands, then into the air, sending it higher each time, until he felt dizzy from craning his head back to track it.

Ronny stuck the hat on his head and tugged it down to his ears. He started to gallop around the yard, pretending to ride a horse. He smiled at Bill and called "Giddy-up," pulling the hat off his head and slapping it against imaginary haunches. Bill smiled in return as he stumbled backwards tracking his highest toss yet. He caught the ball just before he hit the ground. Ronny asked if he was okay. Bill nodded and stood.

The woman in the yellow dress appeared on the back stoop and called to Ronny to come inside. She lingered a moment until she saw Ronny remove the cowboy hat and hand it to Bill.

Bill gave Ronny the baseball.

"I guess I'll see you later," he said.

"Okay." Ronny turned and ran toward the house.

Bill walked back across the vacant lot and up the driveway to the back yard where his father was tending the barrel of burning leaves.

"It smells good," Bill said.

His father nodded. "I know. Nothing like the smell of burning leaves. One of the best signs of fall." With the rake and his free hand, he scooped a pile of leaves into the barrel, sending up fresh plumes of smoke. "Were you playing with Pete?"

Bill shook his head. "I was playing with the new boy, Ronny. His family is the one that moved in over there." He pointed in the direction of Ronny's house.

"Oh, yeah?" His father stood back from the barrel and looked at him. "What did you do?"

"He let me play with his baseball and I let him wear my hat."

"He wore your hat?"

Bill nodded. "We traded."

His father frowned.

"Is that okay?" Bill asked.

His father leaned over and placed his hands on Bill's shoulders. "I don't think you can keep the hat."

"Why? Did I do something wrong?"

"No."

"Then why are you taking my hat away?"

His father's brow furrowed and he let out a sigh.

"We don't know those people, Bill. We don't know anything about them. It's not a good idea to share your hat with someone you don't know." His father gently lifted the hat off Bill's head and dropped it into the barrel. It smoldered but did not burn. Bill stuck his head over the barrel and stared at it, the rising heat warming his cheeks, smoke stinging his eyes. The feeling he had done something wrong gnawed at him. He felt his father's hand on his shoulder.

"I'll buy you a new one," his father said. "I promise."

• • •

The summer after George Floyd's murder, Bill and his wife, Nancy, watched the protest marches on television.

"I know it bothers you," he said, "but we made the right decision."

"Did we?"

"Yes. There are other ways to be involved. We can write letters. We can write checks."

They had agreed to stay home because of Covid, but he could tell she harbored doubts.

"And besides," he said, "Ellen is there. Doesn't that count?"

Their daughter lived in the city and had called to say she and her boyfriend were joining the protest. Bill told her to be careful and to wear a mask. He scanned the crowd shots thinking he might see her. They watched the coverage until past eleven before they went to bed.

He had trouble falling asleep. He lay on his back, staring into the dark. He listened to the hum of the central air, the occasional pop of an air duct, trying to let his mind drift towards slumber.

Instead, he thought of Ronny and the hat. The memory had stayed with him, although he hadn't told the story to anyone except Nancy, when they were in college. They'd been sharing a pizza and drinking beer in a small, dimly-lit café two blocks from campus. He'd been talking about his childhood, describing to this Chicago girl what it was like to grow up downstate, in a town that was mostly white, and ended up telling her about the hat.

"Your dad just threw the hat into the fire?" she asked.

She'd introduced him to *The Autobiography of Malcolm X* and *The Wretched of the Earth*. She talked about racism and the politics of poverty with an earnestness that made him feel shallow and uninformed. She sometimes sat in the student union with a group of Black students whom Bill found slightly intimidating, which in turn embarrassed him because it wasn't as if anyone said or did anything to make him feel unwelcomed. Nancy, with her red hair, blue eyes and creamy white skin, seemed totally at ease. When they first met, he wondered if she had dated any of the guys in the group, but never asked. She always greeted him with a kiss and, as the group's discussion rolled on, rising and falling in intensity, looped her arm through his and leaned closer, displays of affection that reassured him. He loved feeling her pressed against him, watching her face as she spoke. He hoped she could see that he cared about the issues, even if he wasn't as vocal.

"Basically. I mean my mom said something about head lice. I don't know."

"Jesus."

"What?"

"Nothing." Nancy shrugged and took a sip of beer. "You want that?" She pointed to the lone slice of pizza on the tray in the center of the table.

"You think my dad's a racist?"

"I didn't say that..."

"Because he's not. I've never heard him utter a racist word."

"Okay."

"I mean nobody's perfect. You told me your dad voted for Reagan. Twice."

"I said okay."

They split the last slice of pizza and stepped out into the warm spring night. During the walk to his apartment, they were quiet.

Later, lying next to her in his narrow bed, the room lit by a single candle on his dresser, he said he hadn't meant to be so defensive.

She rested her hand on his chest. "Can I ask you something?"

"Sure."

"Why did you tell me about the hat?"

He thought for a moment, watched the play of candlelight on her shoulder.

"I don't know. I think about it sometimes."

"Did you ever play with that boy again?"

"Not really." In fact, he had never played with him again. Ronny was assigned to the other first grade class, which meant they only saw each other on the school bus, in the cafeteria during lunch, and at recess. Bill didn't speak to him past a mumbled "Hi." The following spring, Bill's family moved to a new development on the other side of town.

"That's kind of sad in a way."

"Why?"

"It seems like a lost opportunity. I mean it could have changed your life. Both of your lives."

"Hmmm."

She propped herself on an elbow, looking at him. "I'm serious. We meet people all the time and never know which ones are going to make a difference in our lives."

He nodded. He didn't want to tell her how he had avoided Ronny, or try to explain why. He wasn't sure he could explain the combination of confusion and shame he'd felt toward Ronny after his father tossed the hat into the fire.

Now the air conditioning cut off, leaving the house suddenly quiet. He could hear Nancy's soft, measured breathing. She'd been quiet as they got ready for bed. Once under the covers, she'd read until Ellen texted to say she was safely home, then kissed him good-night and turned off her reading lamp.

"Are you all right?" he'd asked.

"I'm just tired."

"I thought maybe you were upset that we didn't go on the march."

She turned on her side to face him. "I'm upset because of all the craziness in the world right now. Everything is upside down. I feel pretty helpless."

He placed a hand on her cheek. "I love you."

"I love you, too." She kissed his hand. "But I really am tired." She rolled onto her other side. In a moment he heard the sound of her breathing.

• • •

The next morning, he poured a mug of coffee and went to his home office to get on a senior staff call via Zoom. He watched his computer monitor populate with faces in squares like the open-ing of *The Brady Bunch*, except they were all middle-aged white men. There were nods, hellos, bland exchanges of work gossip as they waited for the meeting to start. Then someone mentioned the protest and a few heads started to shake. Bill tuned out the discussion and thought instead of Ellen. He imagined her holding hands with Mark, her boyfriend, and marching in solidarity with the other protesters, believing in something bigger than herself. He heard his name and focused on the screen. Walt, the engineering manager, was smiling.

"I was wondering what you think, Bill, you're the lawyer in the group." Walt said. "Should we defund the police? Do all lives matter or just black ones?" Walt was a stocky, pugnacious man who liked to bait Bill, knowing he was the lone liberal on the staff. When he'd first learned that Bill was a Democrat, Walt had stared at him as if Bill had admitted to being a registered sex offender.

"C'mon, Walt," Bill said.

Walt screwed his pudgy face into a smirk. "What?"

Bill shook his head.

The face of Jack Taylor, the regional VP and general manager, popped onto the screen. "Sorry I'm late, I had an early call with corporate that ran over. What'd I miss?"

"Not much," Walt said, "Bill was just defending rioters." He grinned to let everyone know it was a joke.

"Is that right, Bill?"

"You know me, Jack, I can't resist rousing rabble."

"Right," Jack said. "But we love you anyway." He flashed a smile that radiated warmth and good will. It was a smile, Bill thought, that was either completely genuine, or so well practiced that no one could tell the difference. Either way, Bill succumbed to it every time.

When Jack first joined the company, he'd invited a few members of his staff, including Bill, for a drink after work. Drinks led to dinner and near the end, after the waiter had cleared their plates and brought coffee, Bill and the others listened as their new boss recalled hearing a sports talk radio show one day, when the topic was an NBA player who was the baby daddy to four different women.

"One of the callers, who was obviously a Black guy, he says, 'Frank'—the host's name was Frank—he says," and here Jack slipped into a high-pitched imitation of a Black dialect, "Frank, the boy can't help it. He Black, he Black.'" Jack laughed. Bill's colleagues laughed. Bill smiled and looked at his hands folded on the table.

He'd told Nancy about it when he got home.

"I didn't know if it was some kind of code or a test or something."

"Test for what?" Nancy asked.

Bill shrugged. "Political leaning. How liberal you are."

"Sounds to me like a white guy telling some other white guys a dumbass racist story. Did you say anything?"

"Like what?"

"I don't know. How about 'Not funny?'"

"C'mon, Nancy. I've got to work with this guy."

"So?"

"So, lecturing him about racial sensitivity is not the best way to kick-off our relationship."

She shook her head.

"What?"

"I don't think I could let something like that go."

He'd always thought it was easier for her, a high school social studies teacher in a blue state, to stake out liberal positions, than it was for him, a corporate lawyer.

"Well," he said, "you don't have to."

"But you do?"

"I have to pick my battles," he said.

Now, he listened as Jack ran through the numbers—the monthly update against quarterly targets. The pandemic had knocked business off stride for the current quarter, but if things settled down, they could still hit the annual goal. At the end of the call, Jack asked each of them if they had anything to share with the team.

"Nope, I'm good," Bill said, when Jack called on him.

• • •

At dinner that evening, he told Nancy about his exchange with Walt.

"Didn't you tell me he voted for Trump?"

"Yeah," Bill said. "To be honest, I think most of those guys did, but Walt was the only one who talked about it."

"What an asshole."

"He's a good engineer, and he is not a bad guy to work with, he really isn't. He's actually great to work with. I don't know." Bill took a sip of wine.

"What?"

"I'm always surprised by guys like Walt. I shouldn't be, but I am."

"Did you tell him he was full of shit?"

"No, I decided not to take the bait." He stared at his wine glass. "It's not like I'm going to change their minds. And they're not bad guys, really. Like Jack. First person in his family to go to college, worked his way through. It's what drives him, the belief he's worked hard for everything and doesn't owe anyone. It's the same for a lot of those guys and I kind of admire them in a way. But still..." He shook his head.

"They should know better?"

He nodded. He'd always valued getting along, avoiding confrontation. He'd never asked his father about the hat because he didn't want to have the conversation he knew would follow. He wasn't sure what the point of such a conversation would be. So, he'd left it. His father was not perfect, but he was a good man, and that was enough. It was a judgment he hoped to earn from his own child and from Nancy.

"I'm sorry if I disappoint you."

"Don't do that. Don't put it on me."

"I'm not."

She shook her head. "You kind of are, Bill."

He slumped in his chair, absently swirled his wine.

"I don't mean to put it on you, but it matters to me what you think."

"I think the world is crazy and we all have to do our best to make it less so."

"About me."

"Well," she said, "I think you're intelligent and kind and good looking..."

"C'mon, Nancy."

She leaned closer and placed her hand on his. "I love you, you know that, right? I don't think it's me you have to worry about disappointing."

• • •

The following Saturday, he and Nancy drove into the city to join a protest. They found a parking space in a garage and walked half a mile to the park where protesters were gathering. The crowd was large and growing: men, women, young, middle-aged, Black, white, Asian, parents with children. Bill thought he might be the oldest white man there. Nancy held his hand as they maneuvered into the throng and found a space. After several minutes, they began to march.

They fell in step next to a Black couple. The man was tall and thin, with close-cropped hair gone gray at the temples and black horn-rimmed glasses that gave him a professorial air. The woman was shorter, full-figured, with tightly braided hair that tumbled between her shoulders. When the man caught his eye, Bill nodded. He wasn't sure what to say.

As the march proceeded out of the park onto a wide thorough-fare, he grew conscious of being swept into a sea of strangers drawn together for a single purpose. It struck him how isolated he was in his daily life, how removed he had been, even before the pandemic, from anything as real as this protest.

He thought about the hat, the way it smoldered on top of the burning leaves, the acrid smell, the way his father assumed that a new hat would fix everything. In a way, it did. When his father came home from work that Monday, he presented the new hat to Bill. It was identical to the old one. Bill put it on immediately and wore it until bedtime. His mother even allowed him to wear it at dinner. ("Just this once," she'd said.)

He wore it outside after school the next day. He was going to play with his friend Pete, but as he crossed the front yard he looked across the empty lot. Ronny was in his yard, playing catch with himself as he had been on Saturday. Ronny spotted him and waved. Bill looked at him for a moment, then tugged his hat snugly on his head, turned, and ran the other way.

Now, he wondered what had become of Ronny. He wondered what the odds were that he was part of this march, and if not this one, then another one in some other city. He liked the idea and hoped that it was true.

The protesters moved steadily toward the city center, spanning the thoroughfare from sidewalk to sidewalk. Bill glanced around at the signs held aloft: "Black Lives Matter," "Stop the Hate," "I Can't Breathe," "Silence is Violence." There were chants of "No justice, no peace," shout-outs to various people and the rolling hum of multiple conversations. Bill felt his T-shirt dampen with sweat and took sips from his water bottle. Energized by the crowd and the bright, cloudless day, he turned to Nancy and said he was glad they came. She nodded and smiled but when she didn't loop her arm through his and lean closer, he felt a pang of disappointment.

As they reached the city center, a small group of

counter-protesters wearing red MAGA caps stood along the sidewalk, waving a "Blue Lives Matter" flag and exchanging shouted exhortations and curses with some of the protesters. Bill glanced at them as he passed. Middle-aged men and women, the kind he might see at the grocery store or at a kids' soccer game. One of the men caught his eye, and reflexively Bill started to nod. The man's face dissolved into a scornful glare as he shot his middle finger at Bill and screamed, "Fuck you!"

Bill stared at the man, then started to walk toward him, gripped by an unexpected rush of anger. He imagined ripping the MAGA cap off the man's head and driving his fist into the middle of the man's fat face.

He felt Nancy grasp his hand. "Bill?" When he didn't turn, she tightened her grip and said, "Ignore him."

"He's a fucking asshole."

"I know. Come on." She pulled him back into the flow of the march.

"Hey," Nancy said. "We're doing something good here, right?"

He looked at her. She was smiling, but he could tell he had frightened her. "Right."

"Well then."

He nodded. They *were* doing something good here, or at least something that made him feel good, unlike the hours spent daily in the corporate grind. He made no apologies for the career he had chosen. It allowed him to provide a good life for Nancy and Ellen, and for himself, if he was honest, but he didn't feel like it connected him to anything except his own prosperity.

• • •

On Monday morning he had a Zoom call with Walt to discuss a customer claim stemming from a system outage. The contract gave them air tight protection from the kind of damages the customer was seeking, but that was never the issue. The issue was keeping a good customer happy. Bill and Walt were charged with fact-finding and preparing a briefing for Jack.

Walt popped onto Bill's computer screen wearing a red polo shirt with the company logo. He smiled at Bill, leaned back in his chair and sipped coffee from a company-logoed mug.

"Morning, counselor."

"Hey, Walt. How's it going?"

"Can't complain."

They exchanged bits of small talk. When Walt asked what he had done that weekend, Bill paused for a moment.

"Well, as a matter of fact, Nancy and I went to the protest march in the city."

Walt sat forward, a quizzical smile starting to form on his face. "Is that right?"

"That's right."

Walt chuckled, head slowly shaking. "Well, at least you have the guts to stand up for what you believe in. I can respect that."

Bill hadn't expected anything close to a compliment. "Thanks."

"No, it's true," Walt continued. "I can respect it. I just don't understand it. I mean, whose side are you on?" His voice was not dancing on the edge of sarcasm as it was when he baited Bill. Instead there was concern and a trace of anger.

Bill shrugged. "I believe I'm on the right side, Walt, the side that believes in justice."

"Do you think it's justice to destroy property and steal?"

"There was nothing like that going on this weekend."

"Maybe not, but all you have to do is look at the news to see it is going on all across the country. Thugs smashing windows, looting, burning."

"Are you calling me a thug?" Bill grinned.

Walt rolled his eyes in exasperation. "Of course not. But I do think you're playing right into the hands of Antifa and all the left-wing radicals who want to destroy this country, including most of your precious Democrats."

"Speaking of being played, what do you think your man Trump is doing to everyone who voted for him?"

"Trump," Walt sat up, folding his thick arms across his chest, "is protecting guys like you and me."

"Oh, come on, Walt. Do you really believe that?"

Walt stared at him, round, red face somber, eyes narrowed. "All I know is that this country has been going to hell for a long time. It's not like it was when we were kids. All the things we were taught, respect, patriotism, hard work. They're all gone. We have a goddamn welfare state. Guys like you and me work our asses off so the government can tax half of what we earn to support everyone on welfare and pay for all the government programs that benefit everyone but us. It's a joke."

Bill shook his head. "What the hell does that have to do with the protests?"

"The protests are a symptom of a larger disease."

They were silent. Walt took a sip of coffee. Bill wondered what he could say that would make any difference. Should he tell Walt he was full of shit? After a moment he smiled.

"You'll be pleased to know some guy, a counter-protester, told me to fuck off."

"Yeah?"

Bill nodded. "I wanted to deck him but Nancy pulled me away."

Walt grinned. "Good thing. You're too old to get into fights."

"True," Bill said. "Very true."

• • •

After the call he went to the kitchen to refill his coffee. Nancy was sitting at the kitchen table leafing through notes for her next class.

"It's fresh," she said.

"Thanks. How's your day going so far?"

"Peachy. You?"

"I just got off a call with Walt. I told him we went to the protest and of course that got us off into politics."

She looked up from her notes, a trace of a smile crossing her face. "Did you tell him he was full of shit?"

Bill shook his head. "No, but I did push back on his nonsense. He said I was being played by the radical left, and I told him he was being suckered by Trump."

Nancy considered this for a moment. "Good."

Bill leaned against the counter and sipped his coffee. "He asked me what side I was on. Like we all have to choose sides now. Can you believe that?"

She gathered her notes and stood. "Yes."

"Do you think it's true?"

"I don't know. I hope not."

He thought about his father. Had he chosen sides the day he threw the hat into the fire, or when he moved them to a new neighborhood?

"Me too," Bill said. As Nancy walked past him, he touched her arm. The light from the window caught her pale face, eyes bright blue, streaks of gray in her auburn hair. He stared at her trying to forestall a feeling of sadness. Then he kissed her. Pressing her fingers to his lips, she smiled and continued on her way out of the kitchen.

Triptych

1. Katherine

Katherine Hughes had come to teaching as a way off her father's farm that didn't involve marrying one of the stilted young men who came calling after she graduated high school. She wasn't opposed to marriage, but she didn't want to settle for it.

She'd earned top marks in school, good enough for a partial scholarship to the nearby teacher's college. Her father agreed to pay the rest, once he realized she was not going to accept a marriage offer from any of the local boys waiting to inherit their fathers' farms. "I suppose," he said, "you ought to have something to fall back on."

She loved to read, especially poetry, and imagined meeting a like-minded man, one who loved ideas and literature and could converse about more than crop yields and the price of corn seed.

When she finally met him, he was married.

Now, she woke each morning at 5:00 A.M., lying for a moment under the warm sheets and thick quilt, the room a soft blur until she put on her wire-rimmed glasses. Switching on the lamp, she took her rubber-tipped cane from its place against the nightstand and hoisted herself to a standing position. Steadying herself, she walked to the bathroom, one hand firmly gripping the dark wooden cane, the other on her hip. *An ancient, gray-haired wreck,* she thought, *making ready for another day.*

Eating her breakfast of toast and coffee, she watched the sun come up and thought about the day ahead: five classes of sophomore English at St. Thomas Aquinas Catholic Boys High School. Each one a fifty-minute Sisyphean effort to instill an appreciation of language and literature into 15-year-old boys, to persuade them that Robert Frost and Nathaniel Hawthorne were as worthy of their attention as the Beatles or whatever claptrap they were watching on television instead of reading. Katherine had been pushing the rock up the hill each school year through seven presidents, the Depression, and World War II. First at Sangamon High, the public school, until she reached retirement age, and now at St. Thomas Aquinas, yet she never permitted herself to become discouraged.

She finished her breakfast, rinsed her plate and cup, and went to the living room to wait for Abby. Katherine hadn't driven in years. She took the bus everywhere. There was a stop half a block from her apartment building, and another kitty-corner from the school. But one afternoon in late November, five months ago, Abby Lindstrom, another of the lay teachers at Aquinas, had seen her sitting at the bus stop, pulled her car to the curb, and got out.

"Do you want a ride, Katherine?" she had asked.

"No thank you, dear."

"Are you sure? It's pretty chilly."

"I'm fine. I've been riding the bus for as long as there have been buses in Sangamon."

Abby frowned and sat next to her on the bench.

"Please let me give you a ride, Katherine." She was a sweet young woman, Katherine thought, with a round face and short, lacquered blonde hair. It was meant to be fashionable but Katherine thought instead it made her look older. She gravitated to Katherine in the teacher's lounge during lunch. They were the only women among a dozen priests and two male lay teachers on the faculty, so it was not surprising. While there was something sad about the younger woman that put Katherine on her guard, her pleading expression would have felt cruel to ignore.

"All right," Katherine nodded. "I guess it is a bit chilly."

The following week it snowed. Abby insisted on giving her a ride to and from school. She said it was no trouble, Katherine's apartment building was right on the way. By the time the weather cleared, Katherine found she enjoyed the ease of this new method of commuting. Despite having to sacrifice some of her independence, when Abby suggested they continue the arrangement, she said yes.

Now there was a knock on her apartment door and she gathered her cane and the satchel that served as purse and bookbag and made her way across the room.

"Good morning, Katherine." Abby greeted her with a cheerfulness that was grating so early in the morning.

"Hello, Abby." She stepped into the hallway and locked the door.

"Here, let me get that for you." Abby took her satchel. "It's heavy. I don't know how you carry it." Abby made a similar comment almost every day.

"I'm a country girl," Katherine said. "I am not a stranger to physical labor."

• • •

During their drives to and from Aquinas, Katherine told Abby stories from her forty years of teaching, promising students dropping out of school during the Great Depression to find work to help their families. It was heartbreaking, but what could she say when some families were struggling just to pay rent and buy food?

She did her best to make literature meaningful during such hard times. She tried to show her students the beauty of language and ideas, to instill in them her own love of words and stories, to give them reasons to hope. They didn't have guidance counselors at Sangamon High in those days, but she made herself available to any student, boy or girl, who needed to talk. At the end of each day, she remained seated at her desk grading papers or preparing the next day's lesson. Students stopped by to ask about an assignment or a question from that day's class, but lingered to tell her about a father who lost his job, a mother who cried each night after all the younger children were in bed, a brother who found work in Chicago and could start to send money home. Katherine wanted to comfort them, but felt helpless to do anything more than listen.

When the U.S. entered the war, many of the boys she had taught enlisted. She was not especially religious. She attended Sunday services more out of habit than devotion, but she found comfort seated in the congregation and prayed for those boys, asking the God whose existence she sometimes questioned to keep them safe. A few of them wrote to her, earnest, thoughtful letters couched in boyish language that made her think they'd been forced by dire circumstance to grow up too soon. She wrote them back cheerful letters with news of Sangamon and recommendations of books to read.

Abby must have heard some of these stories before. Katherine had told many of them in faculty meetings or in the teacher's lounge, but the younger woman listened as if hearing them for the first time. She contributed little to their conversations except small talk. This was a relief of sorts as Katherine sensed a pent-up demand in Abby, as if she were waiting for the right moment to unburden herself. Katherine wasn't sure she was ready to listen. She had heard the story: Abby had been engaged to a bright young lawyer named Jeffrey Adams, who died suddenly of a cerebral hemorrhage. He was only thirty-nine.

Abby was asking her a question. "Are you doing the Bryan Joyce reading this year?"

Katherine smiled quizzically before realizing this was another attempt at small talk.

"Of course, dear," she replied. "We hold the reading every year."

Abby turned into the Aquinas parking lot and navigated to a space reserved for teachers. "Good. I always enjoy it."

"I'm glad you do."

"I think it's wonderful to promote the arts and honor the memory of a local poet."

Katherine nodded as she looked at the younger woman. "Well, it is a memory worth honoring."

• • •

She got to her classroom half an hour before the first period bell. She had not been assigned homeroom duties, for which she was grateful. She liked having time to unpack her bag, organize the papers and books, and set the four-foot metal stool in front of her desk on the side nearest the windows. When everything was in order, she sat on the stool, her cane resting within reach against the desk, and waited for the day to begin.

Her classroom was on the first floor, with metal-framed windows that didn't open except for a vent at the bottom, and a view of the school's vast front lawn. At Sangamon High, her classroom had been on the second floor. Its tall windows with wooden sashes lifted easily and faced the frame and red-brick houses with neatly tended yards that had spread out from the center of town—the first neighborhoods of Sangamon. She loved to stand at the windows, the view serene except for the occasional passing car, and the chatter, whoops and laughter of students in the morning and after-noon. After her injury, the principal had offered her a classroom on the first floor, to save her a walk up the stairs, but she didn't want to give up the view, the perch from which she had watched the town grow over the years. She rode the freight elevator instead, chatting with the school janitor, who had the elevator waiting for her each morning and afternoon. He never asked how she'd been injured. Perhaps he'd heard the stories, the rumors that other women might have found daunting. Katherine had heard them and decided the best response was silence.

Now, the bell rang, and she turned on her stool to watch the stream of boys file into the classroom and take their seats. When they had settled, she instructed them to open their textbooks to the section on American poetry. She liked to have the students read aloud, especially when studying poetry. She believed it gave them an appreciation for language, conscious or unconscious. It was an old-fashioned idea, a relic from another time, just like her. The boys in her classes were well-behaved, their upturned faces wore polite expressions, betraying nothing of what they surely were thinking as they regarded her: a wrinkled old woman with a crip-pled knee.

• • •

On the drive home, Abby was subdued. It was mid-April, the time of year, Katherine liked to say, when warm weather, the near-ing prospect of summer vacation, and hormones made teaching most challenging. Perhaps Abby was feeling the strain.

"Long day, dear?" she asked.

Abby nodded, eyes on the road. "Yes."

"Well, it is that time of year. Spring fever. I used to think it was better at Aquinas without the presence of girls to distract the boys, but I am not sure. The distraction seems to be in their heads, no matter where the girls are. What do you think?"

"I guess it is easy to be distracted this time of year." Abby pulled into a space in front of Katherine's apartment building. She got out of the car and retrieved Katherine's satchel from the back seat.

"I really can carry that," Katherine said.

"I know, but I don't mind." She shouldered the satchel and waited for Katherine before starting up the walk to the building. She had the same doleful look as the girls who had lingered next to her desk all those years ago. When they reached her apartment, Katherine asked if she'd like a cup of tea.

After a moment, Abby nodded. "Yes. That would be nice."

When they were seated at the dining room table with their tea, late afternoon light filtering through the window, Abby told her it was the anniversary of Jeffrey's death.

"I still miss him. I always expected to hold him in my memory, but there are days when it feels like I just lost him. I find myself wondering what kind of life we would have had. I'd be a mother by now, I know that. We both wanted children." She shook her head and set her tea cup in its saucer. "Sorry, I'm talking too much. I shouldn't burden you with this."

"We all need to talk sometimes," Katherine said.

"No. I'm just feeling sorry for myself. I suffered a loss, but I have much to be thankful for. Family, friends, a good job. And I am still young. Thirty-six isn't old, is it?"

Katherine laughed. "Good gracious, I should say not. When you get to be my age, you're old. But you, my dear, still have your whole life in front of you."

Abby smiled and started to nod, then put her hand to her mouth, eyes filling with tears. "I'm sorry." Her voice cracked. She wiped her eyes. "I'm sorry."

"It's all right. You needn't apologize."

"I worry sometimes that I had my chance, and now it's gone."

Katherine reached across the table and squeezed Abby's hand. The younger woman attempted to smile, lips pressed together, mouth drawn tightly across her round face. She was living a life she had not imagined for herself, Katherine thought. "I understand," she said quietly, trying to make her voice an instrument of soothing. "But you mustn't give up on yourself."

She remembered standing at the window of her second-floor classroom at Sangamon High the day Bryan died. Had she seen him passing by the school? By then they were little more than acquaintances, or so it seemed to her. They rarely spoke. If they chanced to meet in public, they maintained a strict decorum, but she had seen him, of course she had seen him. She knew his figure—broad shoulders, barrel chest—his striding gait. She'd even glimpsed his face before turning away. That day's mail had included an envelope containing a hand-written copy of a poem with his note scribbled across the bottom. The poem and note were both remembrance and farewell. She'd read them again the next afternoon after hearing the news and wondered what would have happened if she'd lingered at the window, if she'd acknowledged him. She'd thought about it often over the years, even though she knew it was pointless to speculate. Life was full of moments that could have turned one way or the other. The past was a ghost that haunted us if we let it. That's what she should tell Abby, but not now. Now was a time for comfort.

2. Bryan

On the day he died, Bryan Joyce woke half-dreaming of the afternoon he made love to Katherine Hughes in the woods outside Sangamon. More memory than dream, achingly vivid. They'd walked deep into the woods to a spot he knew well. Spread a large down comforter across a patch of ground next to a pond. Ate a picnic lunch of bread and cheese under a canopy of white oaks and sipped from a bootlegged bottle of brandy. He watched her touch her lips after each sip until he caught her hand and kissed her, the liquor sweet on his tongue. When they finished eating, he stood and stripped and waded into the pond up to his shoulders. He turned and called for her to join him. She laughed and shook her head, but he insisted loudly. She took a long swallow of brandy and told him to turn around. He laughed. When he saw she was serious, he turned his back to her until he heard the soft splash of water. He turned and watched her glide towards him, all but her face and pale shoulders under the water. Later they wrapped themselves in the comforter and made love. They stayed until the light began to sink behind the trees. They would have stayed longer except he had a wife waiting at home and Katherine had a reputation to protect. The happiness stirred by the memory quickly turned to melancholy. A gift squandered, like so much of his life.

Now he rose, washed, shaved, and dressed. In his study he retrieved a copy of a poem, wrote a note across the bottom of the page, and folded it into an envelope. Then he took the revolver from his desk drawer and slipped it into the inside pocket of his suit coat.

● ● ●

She'd attended a reading he gave at the auditorium of the new public high school and introduced herself afterwards as an English teacher at the school. Her handshake was firm, although her hand felt soft in his, a surprising and sensual contradiction. Her narrow face was saved from plainness by delicate cheekbones and close-set brown eyes that would not let go of his as she spoke. She told him

185

she admired the imagery in his poems, the cadence of his language, the connection to nature, which she shared. A country girl. After a moment she paused, glanced at the small circle of people that had gathered around them and blushed.

"I'm sorry, I've taken too much of your time."

"Not at all."

"Thank you again. It was a wonderful reading."

Smiling, he made a small bow.

"Miss Hughes," he said as she started to turn away. "If you don't mind waiting for a bit, I'd be happy to resume our conversation."

He could see a shift in her expression, a calculation and then a softening behind her brown eyes. He thought again of how soft her hand felt in his.

"Yes," she said. "That would be lovely."

• • •

He stood on the front porch. Sunlight was creeping up the lawn, which was still half in shadow. An elm dominated one half of the yard. Beneath it was a black wrought iron love seat where he and his wife had sat on summer evenings watching the neighbors pass by. They'd sipped bourbon from the same tumbler; he'd smoked cigarettes. He and Katherine had never sat in the love seat.

• • •

He'd taken her to a café a couple of blocks from the high school. He calculated there was no risk in that. A young school teacher wanted to discuss poetry and literature with a famous local poet and they shared a cup of coffee. What was the harm? She must have felt the same because she didn't object when he proposed it.

They sat at a table in the far corner, away from the door and the large plate glass window on which the name of the café was stenciled in green block letters. When the waitress brought their coffee, he waited for her to leave and glanced around the room before drawing a silver flask from his coat pocket and pouring a dash of whiskey into his cup. Holding the flask over the table, he lifted his eyebrows and nodded at Katherine's cup.

She blushed. "No thank you."

"But you don't mind if I..."

"Not at all."

He smiled, put the flask back in his coat and stirred his coffee. "Good," he said. "I didn't take you for a temperance lady."

"My father liked to keep a bottle of whiskey in the house and have a drink before supper."

"What did he do?"

"Farmer."

"A country girl who became a teacher. Not interested in life on the farm?"

"It's a hard life, especially for a woman."

He nodded. "Yes, but it is important work. Some would even say noble."

"So is teaching."

They talked for two hours. He learned that she had an older brother who was killed in the war, that her father hoped she'd stay and marry one of the local boys and together take over the farm one day. But she had seen how grief and the daily grind of farm life had worn her mother down. She wanted a different life, one steeped in ideas and literature. She loved stories and poems, the life of the mind and imagination, and she hoped to convey that love to her students.

They stayed until the waitress told them the café was closing. Outside, the air was cool and streetlamps cast soft pools of light on the sidewalk. It was past ten o'clock and there were no taxis running. He offered to walk her home. She told him she lived in a rooming house not far away.

"My father also wanted me to join the family business," he said as they walked. "He owned a hardware store. He was very upset when I told him I wanted to go to college. 'A waste of time and money,' he said. "You can imagine what he thought of me becoming a poet."

"Did he change his mind after you started to publish?"

"He died during my second year of college. He left me his house and the hardware store. I sold the store to finance my travel and early writing."

"You quit college?"

He laughed. "Yes. After a year and a half, I decided the old man was right, it was a waste of time and money." A flicker of a frown crossed her face. "For me," he added.

The streets were nearly empty and so quiet they could hear their footfalls. When they reached her rooming-house it was dark except for the porch light. She thanked him for seeing her home, for the coffee and conversation. He made the same small bow as he had earlier.

"The pleasure was all mine," he said. He waited until she was safely inside before walking home. He loved to walk, especially at night when he could lose himself in solitude. He drew the flask from his coat pocket and took a swig.

He passed by dark houses, under the silent sentry of elms and maples, thinking about Katherine, not Miss Hughes. Katherine. Dark eyes flashing intelligence, voice confident and precise, unlike the farm girls he had met in his wanderings. When he reached his house, his father's house, as he still thought of it, all the lights were out, but Thelma would be there, his wife, lying in the dark, waiting for his return. He wasn't sure why. She came from money and defied

188

her father to marry him, a man with no real prospects beyond a modest inheritance, a poet. She was a young woman with no idea of the world who said she loved him, believed in him, and wanted a life with him, consequences be damned. Joyce had rewarded her with debauchery and dalliances. He had loved her, still loved her in his own way, but knew he would lose her when she'd had enough and returned to the father who had not cut her off.

• • •

He headed east toward the center of town, lifting his head to the sun and walking briskly until he reached the small commercial district built around the courthouse square. Crossing the square, he entered the post office, taking the envelope from his breast pocket as he approached the counter.

"Will this go out this morning?" he asked the clerk.

"Yes sir, in about an hour."

"Thank you."

Outside again, he resumed his brisk walk, out of the commercial district in the direction of the high school. He wondered if she would be standing at the window.

• • •

Their affair lasted a year. Their assignations were discreet, passionate and brief. She didn't pressure him to get a divorce, never asked if they would marry. She made it easy for him, and while he was relieved, he was also puzzled.

"Do you ever think of getting married?" he asked her late one afternoon. They were lying under the sheets of a metal frame bed in the cramped room of a motor inn. She lifted her head from his chest and stared at him.

"Are you proposing?"

He met her gaze quietly for a moment. "No, but I sometimes wonder why you spend time and risk your reputation with the likes of me."

"Do you want to stop?"

"No. I just wonder."

Her eyes grew shiny as if she might start to cry and he thought he had gone too far.

"Well," she said, leaning to kiss him. "I guess the life of the mind is not enough."

The sun was setting as they drove back to town. Trees and fence posts shot by as they sped along the narrow road.

"You're going too fast," she said.

"I'm fine." He loved her confidence when they made love, and in her assertion of ideas during their long, languid conversations afterwards, but it rankled him to be criticized.

"Please, Bryan. It frightens me."

"Fear is good. It heightens the senses."

She didn't reply. He glanced at her sitting rigidly, eyes on the road, arm braced against the door. She was terrified. He had gone too far. He reached across the seat and touched her shoulder.

"I'm sorry..."

The car hit a pothole and lurched sharply to the right, careening off the road. He grabbed at the steering wheel and slammed on the brake, cursing as the car smashed into a tree. She screamed once before the impact hurled her against the dashboard.

• • •

She was standing at the classroom window, the angles of shadow and light such that it looked to him as if she suddenly appeared out of thin air. He waited for her to look his way, but she didn't move. She remained still, her gaze fixed, an apparition. Then as suddenly as she appeared, she was gone, stepping back into the shadow of the classroom.

He headed to the edge of town and the old highway. Twice cars slowed and the drivers offered him a ride, but he waved them on. He would walk just as he had all those years ago, when time and the road were his friends, and all that he felt, the lust and fear and wonder, fed the poetry. Words poured out of him as soon as he put pen to paper. Women fell in love with him, indulged him. Even Thelma, the well-bred daughter of a wealthy Chicago banker, abandoned herself to carnality in the first years of their marriage, hoping to appease him. Everything seemed possible until the night he lifted Katherine out of the car and held her, repeating "I'm so sorry," again and again. Standing there in the twilight, the possibility of his own preposterousness first occurred to him.

The accident did permanent damage to Katherine's knee, which had been crushed against the dashboard. It also marked the end of their affair. Whether the injury, which left her needing a cane to walk, made her feel less attractive, or the accident caused her to evaluate the direction of her life, she would not say. She told him simply that she hoped to remain friends, but could no longer see him "in that way."

He came to the woods, and began walking along the old path, glad for the shade, the crunch of dirt and brush underfoot, the sound of birds. He came at last to their place, to the spot under the white oaks next to the pond.

When he returned home from their first tryst, the memory of Katherine emerging from the pond, her voluptuous body like a painting come to life, he wrote a poem about a man and a woman meeting in the woods. It was his favorite of all his poems, not just for the source of its inspiration, but because it marked the beginning of his most productive period.

He had mailed the original draft to Katherine earlier that day, inscribed with a small note. It was the only note he would leave; it was all he had left. He knelt and took the .38 caliber revolver from his coat pocket. Releasing the safety, he sat back and looked at the pond, at the sunlight dancing off the surface of the water, then glanced upward at the sky visible through the leaves, until he felt lightheaded, like the world slipping away. Taking a deep breath, he placed the barrel in his mouth, thinking that he would wait no more for inspiration. He would wait no more.

3. Abby

Abby had no intention of confiding in Katherine. It felt foolish or worse that four years on, she could still feel him, the warm bulk of his body pressed against hers, the palm of his hand on her cheek, the scratch of his beard and softness of his lips when he kissed the hollow of her neck. Jeffrey wasn't the first man she had sex with, but he was the first to make love to her. When she was with him, she let go of doubts about her looks, her body, her awkwardness. For the first few months, she didn't trust the way he made her feel. She was thirty years old and a bridesmaid several times over. Her sister, her best friend from high school, her college roommate. It wasn't going to happen for her. Jeffrey was a nice man, balding and broad-nosed but with kind blue eyes and a warm smile—good-looking in an off-kilter kind of way, which was fine for a man, but not a woman. She liked him from the first time they met, but kept waiting for him not to call. When she realized this wouldn't happen, that he really did think she was beautiful, really did love her, she surrendered her doubts. She believed in the happiness he made her feel. She imagined their life together. Then one Sunday afternoon he complained of a headache, laid down to take a nap and never woke up. She was alone after all.

No, she would not confide in Katherine. No self-pity, which is how it would come across no matter how carefully phrased, and what could Katherine say that hadn't already been said many times since Jeffrey's death? Abby had talked to her mother, her sister, her closest girl-friends, her priest, she'd even gone into therapy for a year. There was nothing left to say, no advice or encouragement she hadn't heard in one form or another. The people in her life were tired of listening and she was tired of talking, of trying to understand why her sadness lingered.

They were unlikely friends. When Katherine came to teach at Thomas Aquinas, Abby was happy to have another woman around besides the school secretary, someone other than the priests and the two men lay teachers to sit with at lunch and during faculty meetings. That was the extent of their interactions. Katherine was polite, even friendly at times, but resisted anything more than a cordial, professional relationship, yet Abby was drawn to her, a woman who had lived independently her whole life. So, one cold November afternoon, Abby saw her sitting at the bus stop and insisted on giving her a ride home. Katherine never took the bus to school again.

During their daily commutes, she regaled Abby with stories from her years of teaching. It seemed like a form of barter at first, entertainment in return for transportation, and though Abby had heard many of them, she was content to listen. Katherine was a natural performer, her face a patchwork of wrinkles with pinkish traces of powder below her jawline. When she spoke, her head wagged slightly side to side as if she were shaking her thoughts loose, and her husky voice and meticulous diction reminded Abby of old actresses in the black and white movies she watched on late night television. Abby realized the stories had another purpose— they kept their conversations from evolving; they held Abby at bay.

The fourth anniversary of Jeffrey's death was a warm, cloudless April day. A day to be reminded that life renews itself, to be happy just to step outside. Instead, Abby was weighed down by thoughts of what she had lost. Katherine's stream of stories and comments were a relief, an excuse not to talk. Then, out of the blue, Katherine asked if she wanted to have tea. Abby hesitated. She'd contained her emotions all day. Wasn't it best to seek the comfort of her own apartment? A place to keep her interminable grief private. Still for the past several months she'd waited for such a gesture from Katherine, a loosening of their elaborate cordiality, a step towards friendship. So, she said yes.

• • •

One Saturday in June, Abby drove Katherine to a beauty salon in downtown Sangamon.

"You're spoiling me," Katherine said.

"Honestly, it's no trouble. You have to get your hair done and I need to do some shopping." This was not strictly true. She didn't need to shop for anything, though now that summer was here she should look for a new bathing suit and a pair of sandals. She enjoyed wandering through Flynn's, the oldest and largest department store in Sangamon. Her mother had taken Abby and her sister there every June to buy one new summer outfit each, and afterwards go to the small café on the third floor for grilled cheese sandwiches and chocolate sodas. She enjoyed checking out the displays and riding the escalator as she had as a child, slowly rising above the glass counters and shoppers, gliding effortlessly until the "big step" at the end, as her mother always reminded her and her sister. Was it sad she found pleasure in such small things? Hopelessly nostalgic? Pathetic?

"I just don't want you wasting your time carrying an old woman around when I can easily take the bus," Katherine said, looking out the window as they passed houses in the older part of town. The noisy hum of a lawnmower broke the morning stillness.

"It's not a waste of my time."

She also liked to browse in the bookstore across from the courthouse. Jeffrey's office had been on the other side of the square and on Saturday mornings she'd pass the time between the bestsellers and classic literature, Harold Robbins and Allen Drury to Charles Dickens and Jane Austen, while waiting for Jeffrey to finish work. She'd sense his presence and turn just as he reached an arm around her shoulder and leaned in to kiss her. Now, on her visits, she found herself lingering in the aisle, pulling a novel from the shelf, examining the cover front and back, waiting for a moment that would never come.

On the day she took Katherine to the beauty salon, she found herself in the poetry section, shopping bag from Flynn's at her feet, looking at a black and white photo of Bryan Joyce on the back cover of a slim volume of his poems. Broad-faced, bearded, dark hair slicked back, eyes peering directly into the camera lens which gave Abby the eerie feeling he was staring at her. She opened the book and flipped through the pages. She had read a couple of his poems in college as part of an American poetry survey course. Despite his local fame, he was a minor regional poet, nothing more. She turned a few more pages to one with a single poem, "Woodland Assignation." It was about two lovers who have come to the woods, the narrator says, "*To reveal ourselves, free of quotidian cares and watchful eyes.*" They undress and swim naked in a pond. The narrator goes first, then watches his lover, "*as in a dream, glide through the water, skin the color of pearl.*"

Closing the book and putting it back on the shelf, Abby remembered the first time she and Jeffrey revealed themselves to each other, undressing in the bedroom of his apartment. She had always been too aware of her body to be comfortable naked or even in a bathing suit, too conscious of her plump figure compared to the girls in high school and college who wore two-piece suits and bikinis. Even her friends who had children seemed to have maintained themselves better than she had. She'd stood anxiously in the pale light seeping from the louvered shade until she saw his expression in the moment before they embraced: wide-eyed, excited, taking her in. An object of desire, like the lover in the poem. Was it wrong to measure herself that way? To feel sad that she may never be looked at that way again? Katherine told her she had her whole life in front of her, but really, wasn't that the problem?

• • •

The Bryan Joyce Memorial Poetry Reading was held in the auditorium of Sangamon High School each July. Katherine organized it, selected and coached each of the readers. Abby volunteered to help, but Katherine, also the caretaker of the Bryan Joyce home, was very proprietary about anything to do with Sangamon's most famous poet. So, from her seat in the front row, Abby watched as Katherine delivered the introductory remarks. Gripping the podium with both hands, her head tilted back and occasionally wagging from side to side for emphasis, she spoke in a firm, clear voice.

"I am older than this building," she said, pausing for the laughter and smiling into the bright light when it came. "And in need of far more repair." She paused again. "Yet I am always made to feel young on evenings such as this. Transformed by the beauty of poetry. I was transformed sitting here forty years ago hearing Bryan Joyce read his poems, and I think it is fitting that we gather here to honor his memory and the art of poetry he loved so much."

Afterward, when the last of the audience had left and the final well-wisher stopped by to offer congratulations to Katherine seated in the lobby, Abby drove her friend home. She thought of her as a friend, even though Katherine still wondered aloud sometimes why anyone as young as Abby wanted to spend time with an old woman.

"I thought it was a lovely evening," Abby said as they pulled out of the parking lot.

Katherine nodded. "It went well."

"All the readers were very good."

"It's a talented group."

"And they had a good teacher."

Ignoring this, Katherine said, "I was especially pleased with the younger readers. It's important to bring along new people each year. What did you think of Thomas Johnson?"

"T.J.? I thought he was excellent. One of the best."

Katherine smiled. "He has a gift. That's what I've told him. He has a gift and he shouldn't waste it."

Abby parked in front of Katherine's apartment building and turned off the engine.

"I'll walk you up," she said.

It was dark except for a pool of light from the street lamp. Going up the walk to the entrance, Katherine took Abby's arm.

"You have gifts too, my dear."

Abby shook her head. "Like the readers? Hardly."

"Perhaps not, but you have others. Your kindness for one."

"That's hardly a gift."

"Oh, but it is. I have seen its absence enough to know it does not come naturally to all people. And you are a good teacher. Very good in fact."

Abby smiled. "Now you're being kind."

"I'm telling the truth."

"Well," Abby's voice trailed off. She wanted to see herself as Katherine did, to see the world as Katherine did. They stood silently for a moment in front of the entry door before Katherine spoke.

"Try not to be so sad, my dear," she said, squeezing Abby's hand. "Nothing good can come of it."

• • •

When Katherine died ten years later, Abby took over as caretaker of the Joyce home and organizer of the reading. In her introductory remarks that year, she mentioned not only Bryan Joyce, but Katherine, recalling how she had been transformed by the friendship of this singular woman and teacher. Eventually, she changed the name to the Katherine Hughes Memorial Poetry Reading.

She was named executor in Katherine's will, and among the belongings, she found an envelope containing a hand-written copy of "Woodland Assignation." She sat at the dining room table in Katherine's apartment and read it, including the inscription at the bottom: "For Katherine, with gratitude and love, Bryan."

She folded the paper and put it back in the envelope. The apartment was as still as a painting. Out the window late afternoon sunlight bounced off the white clapboard siding of the house next door. She didn't feel hurried, even though she still had much to sort through and five classes of freshman English the next day. She smiled to herself and watched the light fade, embracing the solitude.

Grains of Sand

In the spring of 1964, before his mother sent him to one of the bad places, Raymond Lowry was in the eighth grade at Holy Redeemer Catholic grade school. Six foot three inches tall, one hundred-ninety pounds, invariably dressed in brown slacks and plaid shirts buttoned to the top. He stood ramrod straight, towering over his classmates, his posture exaggerated by the habit of clasping his hands together and holding them just above his belt buckle as he talked. He sat in the last desk in the row nearest the windows, his head craning nervously left and right, up and down, sometimes muttering softly to himself until the teacher, Sister Katherine, caught his eye and motioned him to her desk. Raymond obeyed, sliding out of his seat quietly and marching to the front of the classroom, fists balled, arms swinging from his sides.

"Yes, Sister," he whispered loudly, bending so that his face was inches from hers.

"Are you having trouble with the lesson, Raymond?"

"No, Sister."

"Are you sure?"

"Yes, Sister."

"Then why don't you pay attention to doing it rather than look around the room. You're disturbing the others."

"Yes, Sister."

Raymond marched back to his desk, sat, cleared his throat,

and stared at the sheet of paper he had set next to his workbook. It wasn't a lie to tell Sister Katherine that the lesson wasn't giving him trouble, because it wasn't the lesson. Any ninny could do the lesson, even Groucho Marx if he had a workbook which probably he didn't but could if he did. What gave Raymond a problem was trying to figure out how many years were in eternity. He almost had it and was just resting when Sister Katherine called him up to her desk but it wasn't her fault she didn't know. Raymond knew the answer was how many grains of sand times a fraction. Father Owens told them once that if you counted all the grains of sand in the world you would still have only a fraction of the years in eternity. On the paper next to his workbook, Raymond had written: *grains of sand x a fraction.* That was how, but he didn't know how many grains of sand or the fraction. Father Owens hadn't told them probably because he wanted them to figure it out. Maybe Father Owens would tell if he asked and told him he'd tried and got an A for effort except maybe Father Owens didn't know because this was a job for Superman. If he asked in confession it would be a secret.

• • •

On most days, Raymond took books from his desk and opened them, wrote on pages of loose-leaf paper, sometimes handed in assignments. He tried to be part of the class.

One time he was called upon to read a book report aloud. He pinched a piece of notebook paper between the thumb and index finger of both hands as he walked to the front. Facing the class, he made a quick bow and cleared his throat.

"John F. Kennedy will go down in history as one of our greatest presidents. He was a great speaker and saved us from the Cuban missiles. And so, ask not what he can do for you, but what you can do..." Raymond looked up from his paper. His head darted left and right. His lips moved without sound.

"Clang! Clang! Fire on the deck!" Raymond called out suddenly, dropping his arms to his sides. He stood still, a tall and bony human statue with blue eyes staring out of a narrow, acne-covered face.

The class laughed but fell silent when Raymond didn't move. Sister Katherine rose from her desk. "Raymond?"

He blinked and turned his head towards her. "Yes, Sister."

"Thank you, Raymond. You may be seated."

• • •

Raymond lived with his mother in a two-bedroom white rambler. His father did not live with them. Raymond had never met his father.

"He's gone," his mother told him when Raymond was very young.

"Where?"

His mother frowned. "Just gone."

"How long?"

"Forever," his mother said.

• • •

During recess Raymond talked to the classmates who gathered in a semicircle around him. Pacing, bobbing his head, pivoting on his heels so that his whole body turned, chopping the air with his long arms to emphasize a point, he spoke in a voice that ran the scale from bass to falsetto and was punctuated by a laugh that slid unexpectedly into a giggle. He was a source of entertainment to the eighth graders at Holy Redeemer.

"Raymond, do you have any girlfriends?"

"Indeed, I do, Mr. Johnson," he replied, bending from the waist and gesturing towards the girls in the semicircle with a sweep of his arm. "See?"

"Anyone special?"

"We are all special, Mr. Johnson. We are made in the image and likeness of God the Father, Creator of heaven and earth, and of the Son and of the Holy Spirit. Amen. Let us pray." Hands together, eyes shut, lips pursed, thumbs touching the tip of his nose, he looked like an enormous cartoon character poised to dive into a pool.

"Say a prayer for me, Raymond."

Opening his eyes Raymond said, "I will, Mr. Johnson."

• • •

Except during recess at school, Raymond rarely went outdoors. He stayed in his room looking at pictures in the *Life* and *Look* magazines his mother bought and he saved, spreading them on his bed and going through them again and again. He liked the pictures of famous people the best. When he wasn't in his room, he watched television in the living room. He talked to the people on the screen, except when his mother was watching with him. She said it distracted her and told him to stop. His mother never hit him, but when he did something bad, like the time when he was ten and broke her favorite vase, she pinched his ear or his arm, squeezing hard, and scolded, "Now you've done it, Raymond, now you've done it."

• • •

One day at recess, he wandered over to the field where kickball teams were being chosen. He stopped some twenty feet from the edge of the diamond and, head flicking from side to side like a huge bird, observed the scene.

After a moment one of the boys asked if he wanted to play.

"Oh, my gracious no, Mr. Duffy, I don't know how to play."

"C'mon, Raymond, anyone can play kickball."

"But I am not anyone, Mr. Duffy."

It was a hot, cloudless day and every movement stirred little swirls of dust. As the game was underway, Raymond, oblivious to the heat despite his long-sleeved shirt, paced along the side, shouting encouragement and clapping his hands.

"Good catch" he called out, nodding his head vigorously. "Nice pitch, Mr. Conroy," he said when the boy at the plate swung his leg and missed, nearly knocking himself down with the force of his attempt. "Or should I say roll? Oh, never mind, it was nicely done if you ask me."

"Shut up, Raymond," the boy at the plate snapped after he had recovered his balance.

Raymond stopped pacing, stuck his hands on his hips and replied, "Don't be a poor sport, Mr. Warner."

"You're a big turkey," Warner said, pursing his lips and thrusting his head forward in imitation of Raymond.

"That's enough, Michael." Sister Katherine came around the side of the backstop. She stared at him, then looked towards the pitcher's mound. "Let's go, Mr. Conroy."

Near the end of recess, Conroy asked Raymond if he wanted to take a turn.

"Oh no, Mr. Conroy."

"You should take a turn, Raymond," Sister Katherine said, and when he started to object, she raised her hand and shook her head. "No argument."

Raymond nodded and took his position behind the plate, waiting. On the first pitch he kicked awkwardly and sent the ball foul down the third base line.

"We need a hit, Raymond," Conroy called to him. "Just get on base."

Raymond looked at him for a moment, then turned to the pitcher, who drew his arm back and rolled the ball towards home plate. Raymond, head down, arms flapping like a bird getting ready to take off, ran to meet it and in one swift motion of his long right leg, sent it flying over the head of the pitcher and Warner, playing second base, and the center fielder, who had moved in expecting a grounder.

"Run, Raymond," Conroy shouted.

Awkward for the first few steps, Raymond found his stride halfway to first base. He ran like a wild ostrich, arms pumping, legs devouring the base path in huge strides. As he reached third, head held erect, face flushed, his teammates shouted and waved him home. By then the center fielder had retrieved the ball and relayed it to Warner, who, turning and seeing Raymond round third, ran straight toward him. Halfway across the infield, ten feet from Raymond's back, Warner hurled the ball violently, his momentum rocking him forward several steps.

The ball hit Raymond on the back of the head, knocking him to his hands and knees.

"He's out!" Warner yelled.

"Are you all right, Raymond?" Conroy asked.

Sister Katherine hurried toward Raymond.

Raymond stood up, his face as red as a fever. Suddenly he lunged forward, wrapped both hands around Warner's neck and shook him. Warner danced on his tiptoes, eyes bulging, frantically clutching at Raymond's arms.

"Stop it!" Sister Katherine yelled, grabbing Raymond's shoulders.

Raymond released his grip and turned to her with a startled look, as if waking from a dream. Warner stumbled backwards, coughing.

The recess bell rang.

• • •

At Sunday mass, Raymond and his mother sat near the back of the church on the end of the pew next to the side aisle. Easier to slip out if Raymond could not control himself, if his voice rose and his body rocked forward and back. There were times when his mother had to pinch him to still his mumbling. When he shut his eyes, his long fingers pressed together evenly in a perfect attitude of devotion, she'd let go. Other times he disappeared into himself, staring silently. When he came back, blinking, she'd touch his arm to soothe him. Sometimes, parishioners in the neighboring pews looked at them with annoyed expressions. Raymond's mother met and held their stares until they looked away.

One Sunday a few weeks before the incident with Michael Warner, Raymond was mumbling and rocking in the pew. His mother whispered to him to settle down, and when he ignored her, she gripped his arm, not a pinch, but a firm grasp just above his elbow. He glared at her and hissed, "I'm talking to God!" Startled, she patted his arm, "Okay, okay." He faced front again, calmer, folded his hands, closed his eyes and returned to his prayer. He'd been asking God to help him figure out the grains of sand.

Mrs. McGill, a retired teacher at Holy Redeemer, was sitting behind them as she did every Sunday. After mass ended and parishioners were filing out, she leaned over the pew and asked in a soft voice, "Are you all right?"

"I'm sorry," Raymond's mother said. "I don't know what got into him. He can be a trial sometimes."

205

Mrs. McGill nodded. "Have you thought of getting help?"

"He's a good boy."

The older woman took her hand, brow furrowing beneath her wispy white hair. "I know you love him, but you need to be careful. He's going to get beyond you one day."

"He's not a burden," Raymond's mother said.

They knew the Warners from church. Every Sunday they marched up the center aisle nodding and smiling at the other parishioners. "Just like the Pharisees," Raymond's mother said to him.

Mr. Warner had come to their house one evening a few years earlier and asked to speak to Mr. Lowry.

"There is no Mr. Lowry," Raymond's mother told him.

"Can I help you?"

"Oh, well." He was embarrassed. "It's about the church building fund."

She invited him in and offered him coffee. He sat at the kitchen table with his coat on, as if he might have to leave at any moment. She pledged one hundred dollars which he said was more than generous. "How much more than generous?" Raymond asked. He was tall even then, an exotic, red-faced bird.

Now Raymond's mother told him about the meeting she'd had with the Warners and Father Owen, the pastor at Holy Redeemer. The Warners were upset about what happened to Michael, she said. She said there were people who wanted to take him away if he wasn't good.

"Take me where?" he asked.

"A bad place."

"Like hell?"

"Yes," she said. "So, you must be good. Do you understand, Raymond? You must be good or they'll make me send you to one of those places."

Raymond blinked, nodded. Blinked again.

• • •

In the fall of 1964, the boys from Holy Redeemer entered St. Thomas Aquinas High School with the boys from the other Catholic grade schools. Raymond walked the hallways with his books clutched to his chest, head turning from side to side and nodding slightly as he walked, like he was trying to count everyone he passed. He was not in any classes with the boys from Holy Redeemer, but he had gym and the same lunch period as some of them, including Conroy and Warner. Raymond sat by himself at the end of a table next to the wall. He set his lunch bag on the table, removed the items one at a time and placed them in a straight line. He ate methodically, taking a bite from each item—sandwich, chip, carrot, sandwich, chip, carrot. The sound of voices, laughter, slap of hands on tabletop, belches, and metal chair legs scraping linoleum rolled in waves across the cafeteria, but he did not look up. Sandwich, chip, carrot. Suddenly a crumpled ball of aluminum foil hit the edge of the table with a thud. Raymond's head snapped up and craned right and left like a startled turkey. He saw Warner seated a couple of tables away, laughing. Raymond blinked several times before going back to his lunch.

Sandwich, chip, carrot.

• • •

Coach Murkowski did not make Raymond dress for gym class. He was allowed to stand to the side with the boys who had doctor's notes excusing them from participation. Raymond did not have a note. On the first day, he had stood outside the locker room while the other boys filed inside.

"Is there a problem?" Coach Murkowski had asked.

Raymond looked at him wordlessly.

The coach, as tall as Raymond, stood just inside the locker room, holding the door ajar with one foot. "What's your name, son?"

"Raymond Lowry."

"Well, Mr. Lowry, gym class is starting, you need to get inside and get dressed."

"Are they taking their clothes off?"

Coach Murkowski nodded. "Yes."

Raymond folded his arms across his chest. "I cannot take my clothes off."

"I know some boys are a little shy, self-conscious, but..."

"I cannot take my clothes off." Raymond's voice was a pleading whisper, his blue eyes wide.

Coach Murkowski stepped into the hallway, the door clicking shut behind him. He looked at Raymond, saw his lower lip quiver.

"It's okay, son, you don't have to dress. But you need to come outside and get some fresh air."

Coach Murkowski held the door for Raymond, who entered the locker room with his hands held to each side of his head like blinders, and crossed to the door on the other side that opened onto the athletic field.

• • •

On Thursday of the second week of school, a group of boys, including Warner, stood on the edge of the athletic field talking as Raymond approached. He wanted to stand next to the building, but Coach Murkowski told him he had to take the field with the other boys. Except for Raymond, they all wore navy blue gym shorts with "St. Thomas Aquinas High School" etched in a white circle on the left thigh, and white T-shirts. Patches of clouds cast irregular shadows on the worn grass.

"Nice gym clothes," said one of the boys.

"He doesn't dress for gym." Warner put his hands to the sides of his head as he had seen Raymond do when walking through the locker room. The other boys laughed.

Raymond stood quietly, hands at his sides.

"What's the matter, Raymond?" Warner asked. "Are you afraid you'll get a boner?"

Warner stepped toward Raymond.

"Is that it? Scared of getting a boner?"

Raymond pressed his hands over his ears.

"You do know what a boner is, don't you? You do have a dick?"

Raymond held his hands tightly against his ears and started to shake his head and hum. As the boys formed a semicircle around him, he shook his head faster, the sound of his hum piercing the air like the drone of a small engine.

"Boner!" Warner shouted at him and the other boys joined in a vicious chorus.

"Boner! Boner! Boner!"

Raymond's hum grew into a low animal sound. He dropped his hands from his ears and started to rotate, swinging his arms and fists like a medieval war machine. He swung wildly, hitting one boy on the side of the head with unexpected force. He caught Warner on the nose and sent him stumbling backwards, blood spurting. He screamed and swung and swung, until Coach Murkowski came running. Conroy came right behind him. Together they wrestled Raymond to the ground. Raymond's acned face was swollen and red as he mumbled to himself.

"Now you've done it, Raymond," he repeated. "Now you've done it."

• • •

Raymond's mother sat next to him on the sofa in the living room. He sat very straight, hands folded on his lap. Gray afternoon light from the picture window left the room shadowy, but caught his eyes, which seemed not to move or blink.

"Father Ryan won't take you back, Raymond. He says you are not a good fit at St. Thomas Aquinas. It's not like Holy Redeemer. He wants me to put you in one of those places. What are we going to do?"

Raymond stirred. He pressed his folded hands to his chest and started to rock gently forward and back, whispering.

"What is it?" his mother asked.

Raymond stared out the picture window. "Now you've done it, Raymond," he said. "Now you've done it."

"Yes, you have," she said. "You really have done it this time. I told you what would happen if you weren't good."

He rocked forward and back and spoke louder. "Now you've done it, Raymond. Now you've done it."

She touched his arm. "It's all right."

"Now you've done it, Raymond."

She rubbed his arm. "Shhh, Raymond, it's all right—"

"Now you've done it." His long body rocked violently, the back of his head banging against the wall.

"Raymond?" She grabbed at his shoulder.

"Now you've done it!" he screamed, his trembling, scarlet face close to hers, eyes boiling.

Raymond's room had a window and a bed, but no desk or paper or pencils. The window was small and square and had steel bars in front. There was a tree outside and sometimes he saw birds.

When his mother came to see him, they went to a different room and sat in large chairs facing each other. His mother didn't say much, except to tell him it would be all right. This was their cross to bear, but God had a plan.

Each day a man came to talk to him. He spoke in a calm voice that reminded Raymond of Father Owens.

"Do you know where you are, Raymond?" he asked each day.

"Of course, don't you?"

"Where are you, Raymond?"

"In a room."

The man nodded. "Do you know where the room is?"

Raymond thought it was some kind of puzzle.

"You're in a hospital, Raymond."

Raymond pursed his lips and rocked. The man wrote something on a pad he held on his lap. Raymond couldn't see what he wrote but he did it every time they talked. Maybe he was writing down answers. Maybe he knew about the grains of sand.

Acknowledgments

First, my thanks to Apprentice House Press for believing in this collection, and to Matthew McCarney, Molly Clement and Olivia DiTroia for guiding me through the publication process. I had a lot of help writing these stories. I am grateful to the Writer's Center in Bethesda, MD for providing a space where writers can meet and develop their craft; to Dana Cann, Dan Gutstein, Julie Lin Wakeman, the late Ann McLaughlin, and Virginia Hartman for excellent writing workshops; to Dave Housley for thoughtful comments, encouragement and always replying to my emails; to the members of my writers' group: Liz Kirby, Sylvia Karman, Mladena Vucetic, Christina Nelson, Sarah Tascone and Ruben Castaneda, for helpful insights and lively discussions. I owe a special debt of gratitude to John Morris, whose generous and incisive comments inform all the stories in this collection. I am grateful to my daughters, Dorothy and Sarah, for their love and support. Finally, to my wife, Susan—thank you for everything over all the years we have been together. You make it matter.

About the Author

David C. Metz's stories have appeared in several literary magazines, including *The MacGuffin*, *New Plains Review*, *Bull*, *Valparaiso Fiction Review* and *Perceptions*. Originally from Illinois, he lives with his wife in Damascus, Maryland.

Apprentice
House Press
Loyola University Maryland

Apprentice House is the country's only campus-based, student-staffed book publishing company. Directed by professors and industry professionals, it is a nonprofit activity of the Communication Department at Loyola University Maryland.

Using state-of-the-art technology and an experiential learning model of education, Apprentice House publishes books in untraditional ways. This dual responsibility as publishers and educators creates an unprecedented collaborative environment among faculty and students, while teaching tomorrow's editors, designers, and marketers.

Eclectic and provocative, Apprentice House titles intend to entertain as well as spark dialogue on a variety of topics. Financial contributions to sustain the press's work are welcomed. Contributions are tax deductible to the fullest extent allowed by the IRS.

To learn more about Apprentice House books or to obtain submission guidelines, please visit www.apprenticehouse.com.

Apprentice House Press
Communication Department
Loyola University Maryland
4501 N. Charles Street
Baltimore, MD 21210
Ph: 410-617-5265
info@apprenticehouse.com • www.apprenticehouse.com

www.ingramcontent.com/pod-product-compliance
Lightning Source LLC
Chambersburg PA
CBHW051341020726
47501CB00007B/2204